"Do you feel it?"

"Feel what?"

"Someone watching." She tipped her head back to see his sharp gaze swinging back and forth. He was looking, too. "Do you think I'm paranoid?"

That clear blue gaze settled on her. "No. I've felt it, too." His hands tightened at her waist and he pulled her into his chest, winding his arms behind her back and resting his chin at the crown of her hair.

Her arms caught between them and she whispered against the KCPD logo embroidered on his chest. "Did you see someone? What do you need me to do?"

"Easy, partner. I need you to let me hold you for a minute. Okay?"

Hope nodded. She willed herself to relax against him. "I'm okay with that."

"You're not alone, Hope. It's you and me, remember? This guy's going to try to come after you, but he won't get to you, understand? I won't let him."

Whatever the reason behind this show of support, Hope curled her fingers into the back of his shirt and held on. She needed to feel safe for a few moments. She needed to know she'd made the right decision to agree to helping the police.

She needed to hear him say it again, in that deep, husky voice that danced across her eardrums and soothed the fear from her heart. "You're not alone."

TASK FORCE BRIDE

USA TODAY Bestselling Author
JULIE MILLER

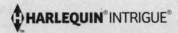

For the wonderful pets who have blessed my life:
Purr, Bobbi, Boots, Frosty, Cocky, Peanut Butter,
George, Anxious, Butterscotch, Reitzie, Duke, Patches,
Sherlock, Shasta, Padre, Maxie and Maggie.

Recycling programs
for this product may
not exist in your area.

Please consider supporting your local animal shelter,
and open your heart to a new furry friend.

ISBN-13: 978-0-373-69711-3

TASK FORCE BRIDE

Copyright © 2013 by Julie Miller

Printed in U.S.A.

ABOUT THE AUTHOR

USA TODAY bestselling author Julie Miller attributes her passion for writing romance to all those books she read growing up. When shyness and asthma kept her from becoming the action-adventure heroine she longed to be, Julie created stories in her head to keep herself entertained. Encouragement from her family to write down the feelings and ideas she couldn't express became a love for the written word. She gets continued support from her fellow members of the Prairieland Romance Writers, where this teacher serves as the resident "grammar goddess." Inspired by the likes of Agatha Christie and Encyclopedia Brown, Julie believes the only thing better than a good mystery is a good romance.

Born and raised in Missouri, this award-winning author now lives in Nebraska with her husband, son and an assortment of spoiled pets. To contact Julie or to learn more about her books, write to P.O. Box 5162, Grand Island, NE 68802-5162 or check out her website and monthly newsletter at www.juliemiller.org.

Books by Julie Miller

HARLEQUIN INTRIGUE

CAST OF CHARACTERS

Hope Lockhart—Wedding planner and owner of Fairy Tale Bridal Shop. A shy, secretive woman who makes happily-ever-after's happen for everyone else. After escaping a close encounter with the Rose Red Rapist, the neighborhood spinster becomes the task force's best chance at capturing him. But agreeing to be the bait in KCPD's trap means facing off against her own private fears... and a man who wants her dead.

Edison "Pike" Taylor—K-9 cop with KCPD. Nobody protects and serves Kansas City the way a Taylor can. This neighborhood cop has got his work cut out for him when he's assigned to go undercover as Hope's fiancé. Teaching the inexperienced Hope how to act like a woman in love is challenging enough. Keeping her alive might be the toughest—and most important—mission this cop could have.

Hans—Pike's canine partner. A well-trained officer who likes playing tug-of-war and chasing down bad guys.

Hank Lockhart, Sr.—Hope's father wants his daughter's forgiveness.

Nelda Sapphire—Hank's girlfriend.

Brian Elliott—Hope's mentor and friend. His vision for revitalizing downtown KC doesn't include a serial rapist.

Adam Matuszak—Hope's attorney. Where do his loyalties really lie?

Leon Hundley—The neighborhood handyman has fixed a lot of things in Hope's shop.

Gabriel Knight—Reporter at the *Kansas City Journal*. What's his deal with KCPD, anyway?

Vanessa Owen—Television news reporter. She's got the lead on a story that could make her a star.

The Rose Red Rapist—Will he finally be brought to justice?

Prologue

Today was a bad day to be a bride.

"Hello?" Hope Lockhart pressed her phone to her ear and inched her way toward the door, quietly seeking an escape as her perfectly executed plan for her client's wedding blew up in an explosion of harsh words and wailing tears. "Hello?"

Click.

Hope cringed as the mysterious caller hung up without saying a word. She didn't need this today. She tucked her phone into the hip pocket of the gray suit she wore and hurried her steps.

"Cold feet is not an option, young lady," Dale Barrister lectured his daughter over the chamber music drifting down from the sanctuary upstairs while the mother of the bride wept right alongside her daughter. He pointed his white-gloved finger to the ceiling. "Everyone who's anyone in Kansas City is in that church right now, waiting for us."

"Daddy!" Deanna Barrister wailed, pushing her veil away from the mascara running down her cheeks. "I don't think I can do this. Not today."

"Well, we're not doing it tomorrow or any other day." The skin above his starched white collar turned red with anger. "I spent more money on this shindig than you're worth, and this is how you repay me?"

Hope curled her fingers around the doorknob behind her and paused at the cruel words. Raised voices always twisted her stomach into knots. Tension like this usually suffocated the breath from her chest and scattered coherent thoughts right out of her head. The anger, pain and frustration filling the room reminded her of things she'd worked long and hard to forget.

"You stupid cow! When I tell you to do a thing, I expect—"

Uh-uh. Hope slammed the door on that particular memory and forced herself to take a deep breath and intervene. "Mr. Barrister, perhaps if we give Deanna a few minutes—"

"Miss Lockhart!"

It wasn't a great day to be a wedding planner, either.

Hope flattened her back against the door as the father of the bride whirled around and stalked across the dressing room toward her. "I'm paying you a boatload of money."

She turned her head from the finger jabbing near her face.

"You make today happen."

As much as every frayed nerve inside her longed to bolt to a place of silence and solitude, she'd also worked long and hard to learn how to cope with volatile emotions and uncomfortable situations like this. She was stronger than her past. She could do this. Her client needed her. And if someone needed her, she had to help. That had always been her Achilles' heel. Hope released the door, keeping her voice calm and her smile serene.

"Of course." She gestured to the woman wiping at the tears that dripped on her taupe lace gown. "Perhaps you could take your wife to the restroom to freshen her face," she suggested, needing to clear some of the emotions from the room if she was to have any chance of saving the big day. Ignoring both the father's impatient curse and the doubt in the reluctant bride's red-rimmed eyes, Hope pulled out her phone and texted her assistant upstairs. Tell organist to play another 15 min. Send groom down. Keep smiling. Pray.

Hope hit Send and looked up to see the fractured family all staring expectantly at her. A mixture of compassion and trepidation filled her. She'd worked miracles in the past to make a bride's wedding dreams come true. She hoped she had another miracle up her sleeve today. "Mr. Barrister? Please."

With a grunt and a nod, he swung open the door and pulled his wife into the hallway with him. Hope closed the door softly, studying the grain in the fine old walnut, racking her brain for the next step in this impromptu wedding rescue.

A soft sniffle from the young woman behind her provided an inspiration. Adjusting her narrow-framed glasses on the bridge of her nose, Hope spotted a box of tissues on a shelf and retrieved them before sitting in the Sunday school chair beside her client. "Here."

Deanna pulled a handful of tissues from the box to wipe her face and blow her nose. "It's too much. I can't take this kind of pressure. What if I'm wrong?"

"About Jeff?"

"About getting married. I'm only twenty-two."

A decade younger than Hope. Her client had so much life ahead of her. She had two parents who loved her, even if they were having a hard time expressing it on this particularly stressful day. She was slender, beautiful—stunning in the mermaid-style gown Hope had helped her select. Deanna had a handsome young doctor who wanted her to be his wife.

Not for the first time in her life, a pang of envy nipped at Hope's thoughts. And not for the first time, she pushed aside that longing and focused on what needed to be done at that moment.

She found a discarded florist's box for Deanna to toss her soiled tissues into, and offered her another handful as the tears quieted into silent sobs. "You know, Deanna," Hope began, "today isn't about those people upstairs. Or the gifts or the doves or the champagne we'll serve at the reception. It isn't about how worried your father is that this won't turn out to be the happiest day of your life."

"He just wants it to be over."

"He wants it to be perfect. He's about to lose his little girl to another man, and today is his way of showing the world how much he loves you and how much he's going to miss you. He's worried that you won't be happy."

"Dad's angry with me, not worried. Today is a business opportunity for him, publicity for his company. He doesn't care what I'm feeling."

Hope's phone vibrated with an incoming call, setting off a chain reaction of startled gasps. She apologized before reading the incoming number, and then felt the warmth drain from her blood. How? Why? She had a pretty good idea who the unknown caller harassing her today might be. The Fates must be mocking her for sitting here and defending fathers.

"Do you need to take that?"

"No." Hope purposefully ended the call as temper brought heat back to her body. She'd have to change her cell number. Again. She buried the phone in her jacket pocket, politely masking the urge to hurl it across the room. Hope inhaled a deep breath and remained calm for the woman beside her. "Some men—some people—don't know how to express what they're feeling in a way we all understand. For fathers, I think the wedding day is that one last hurrah that he can do for you. He's trying to show his love by giving you everything he thinks you want. But I'm guessing—behind the frustration and anger—that he's afraid."

Deanna sniffed. "Of what?"

"That he's failed you. That if he'd done something more or less or different, then you wouldn't be having second thoughts about getting married."

Deanna blinked a few last tears from her dark brown eyes and looked at Hope. "Dad never failed me." Lucky woman. "It's just that today has gotten so out of hand. There's so much that has to happen."

"There's only one thing that has to happen." Hope reached over and patted Deanna's hand. "Don't think about the pressures of the day—that's what I'm here for. Think about yourself, and the future you'll have with your husband."

A soft knock at the door ended the conversation. "Dee?" The groom covered his eyes as Hope let him in. "Your dad said you were freaking out. Is everything okay?" he asked, peeking between the fingers of his crisp white gloves.

Hope pointed to the woman rising to her feet. "I thought maybe you two could use a quiet minute alone."

He dropped his hand and turned to his bride-to-be. "Wow."

Deanna blushed at his unabashed appreciation for the image she created in the subtly blinged gown she wore. "Jeff. You shouldn't see me before the wedding."

"There *is* going to be a wedding, right?"

Hope politely faded into the woodwork when the bride's and groom's eyes locked onto each other's. There was so much love, acceptance and desire in Jeff Stelling's eyes that she didn't see how any woman could hesitate to commit to a man who looked at her that way.

"That's all that has to happen today." Deanna repeated Hope's words and met her fiancé in the middle of the room. "You and me. I want to spend my life with you."

"I love you, Dee. Come upstairs and start that life together with me. Please?"

"I love you." He leaned in for a kiss before Deanna shooed him out. "Okay. Go up to the church. Tell Dad I'll meet him upstairs. Hope? Can you make me gorgeous again in five minutes?"

Crisis averted. Tally up one more happily-ever-after. For someone else. The phone was vibrating against her hip again. Her past was calling. Ignoring it, Hope smiled. "You bet."

Chapter One

"Really?" Hope squinted and averted her eyes from the bright headlights that filled up her rearview mirror. "You're following a little close, buddy."

She gripped the steering wheel more tightly and pressed on the gas to put some distance between them. She wasn't a nervous driver at all. But normally she wasn't out this late, and she didn't take the shortcut off the interstate through the heart of the city. But cleanup after the Barrister-Stelling wedding had run long past the end of the dinner and dancing. And though she wasn't the one actually bussing the tables, there were family pictures and table decorations she'd promised to hold on to until after the honeymoon. Then the gifts had to be delivered to their parents' hotel rooms. Other than the hotel staff, she'd been the last person to leave the reception.

So what if her panty hose had long since cut off the circulation to her toes? Or if she'd have to unload every last box in the trunk and backseat of her car herself because she'd sent her assistant home. Hope had earned a tidy fortune with this event. Earned every last penny playing fashion consultant, wedding planner and family counselor. The sooner she got home, the sooner she could celebrate with a glass of wine and a long, hot bubble bath. Or maybe she'd skip them both and just fall straight into bed and sleep until Monday.

"What the heck?"

The same lights rushed up behind her a second time, nearly blinding her. "Jackass."

Hope blamed the unlady-like condemnation on the length of the day and the unwanted calls piling up on her cell phone that bothered her more than she cared to admit. She must have a stamp on her forehead that said "Pick on me" today. Just because she tended to be shy and soft-spoken didn't mean she lacked backbone or a brain or a temper. When the driver flashed his lights through her rear window, she muttered another word in the Ozark accent that crept into her voice whenever she got a little too angry or afraid. She double-checked her speed. She wasn't poking along, by any means. Still, if the guy was in that much of a hurry…

Pulling closer to the parking lane so he could pass, Hope adjusted her charcoal-framed glasses to try to catch a look at the driver and license plate on the beat-up white van. But it veered so close as it sped past that it nearly clipped the side mirror on her car. "Hey!"

The van shot back into the lane in front of her, forcing Hope to stomp on the brake and skid to a stop. Glass rattled and boxes shifted behind her as several brief images printed like snapshots in her brain. A shadowy figure dressed in dark clothes sat behind the steering wheel. He wore a black knit cap pulled low over his forehead and a white scarf across his nose and mouth, hiding all but his eyes. In those brief milliseconds when he'd looked down into her car, she was certain their gazes had met, although he flew on by before the details completely registered. A shiny silver bumper that seemed at odds with the rusting wheel wells and dinged-up back doors was the last image she saw before it disappeared into the night.

"Where's a cop when you need one?" She sighed, fighting a niggling sense of unease that her sleep-deprived brain was keeping her from recognizing something important.

"Need some help, sugar?" A trio of young men, dressed in hoods and jeans and more jewelry than she owned, knocked on her passenger-side window.

Startled by their approach and frightened by their leering smiles, Hope stepped on the accelerator and did a little speeding herself—leaving a trail of rubber, laughter and catcalls in her wake.

She drove three more blocks before she eased up on the gas. Hope inhaled a deep breath and ordered herself to get a grip. It was probably just the neighborhood she was driving through that had made her suspicious of the van and driver. Besides the three young men, she'd passed a homeless man pushing his cart along the sidewalk, and at least one scantily clad woman who'd been leaning into a parked car—either picking up a client, making a drug buy or both.

If Hope wasn't so darned nearsighted, maybe she could have read the van's license plate, even on the dimly lit street. If she wasn't so distracted by those unwanted phone calls, she could have gotten a useful description of the driver. If she wasn't so worn-out, maybe she would have taken the long way home and bypassed this run-down neighborhood where she had no business driving alone, anyway.

Hope breathed a sigh of relief as she finally left the less savory section of the city behind her and drove past the familiar landmarks of renovated art deco build-

ings, solid midcentury brownstones and converted
warehouses that now housed trendy new businesses
and condo apartments like her own. Her company improved, too. Instead of the prostitute and gangbangers,
and rude drivers crowding her on the street, she drove
past a busy bar with a neon green shamrock sign and a
group of friends standing outside the front door, shar-
ing a laugh and a smoke.

She stopped at the next light and waited for a young
twentysomething couple to cross in front of her. They
were holding hands, out on a Saturday night date to a
restaurant or coffeehouse in the next block. Or perhaps
they were meeting a group of friends to go dancing at
one of the newly opened clubs in the trendy Kansas City
neighborhood where Hope lived over her own shop.

A little pang of longing squeezed at Hope's restless
heart. Even if she had a date, or a whirlwind social
life that included dancing and barhopping, she was too
tired to do more than drive herself home tonight. She
couldn't wait to kick off her heels, slide into that bath
and curl up with a good book.

Still, it would be nice if just once she had something
more to look forward to than a hard day of work and
a quiet night at home. She wanted something more—
something a little more exciting, something a little less
lonely.

Almost as soon as she thought the wish, she regret-
ted it.

She knew she was lucky to have built a successful
business. Lucky to have a solid roof over her head and
plenty to eat every day. She was lucky to have a few
friends and a younger brother she was so proud of serv-
ing in the Marines. Hope's gaze dropped to her right
hand where it rested on the steering wheel. A familiar

web of pale scar tissue peeked above the cuff of her tan trench coat. She touched her fingers to the collar of her silk blouse, knowing there was more scarring underneath. All along her arm, her foot, her thigh—there were scars there, too.

She was lucky to be alive.

Hope was grateful to be where she was now, considering where she'd started. She was pushing her luck to dream of something more—like holding hands or being the recipient of a look like the one Jeff Stelling had given his bride, Deanna, today.

"Damn lucky," she whispered out loud as the light changed. And she meant it. As long as other people kept falling in love, she'd have a job—and the security she'd been denied growing up. What would she do with a man, anyway? Embarrass herself? Shy, plump and partially disfigured—what man wouldn't want to get all over that?

With a healthy dose of mental sarcasm to sharpen her dreamy focus, Hope turned onto her street. The familiar brick facade and storefront windows she'd decorated herself welcomed her as she slowed to pull into the parking lot beside Fairy Tale Bridal.

Hope parked her car in the reserved space next to the side entrance and climbed out, keys and pepper spray in hand. As stylish and reborn as this neighborhood might be, it, unfortunately, had become the hunting ground of a serial rapist that the press had dubbed the Rose Red Rapist. She had the unwanted distinction of being responsible for the horrid nickname because one of his first victims had been abducted right outside her shop. So much for fairy tales. Several more women, including a friend who'd worked just across the street at the Robin's Nest Floral shop, had been blitz attacked, driven to another location, sexually assaulted and then dumped back here on this very block as if they were so much trash.

A client of hers, Bailey Austin, had been that first victim. Hope still felt guilty about the night more than a year ago when Bailey—then an engaged woman having a tiff with her fiancé at the shop—had stormed out of Fairy Tale Bridal and been assaulted. Although the younger woman had assured Hope that she in no way held her responsible for the attack, Hope was still looking for a way to make restitution.

Hope unlocked the vestibule and picked up the mail off the floor that had come through the slot. Then she unlocked the inner door to her shop and set the bills and letters along with her purse inside before returning to her car to unload the boxes from the wedding reception. She tilted her gaze to make sure the security lights and camera monitoring the entrance were working before opening her trunk and grabbing the first box of family mementos from her car.

With each trip to and from the shop, she made a point of scanning her surroundings and locking her car. KCPD had formed a task force to track down and arrest the elusive rapist, and they had stepped up patrols in this particular neighborhood. The Rose Red Rapist had received plenty of press on television and in the local papers, although facts about the attacks often got less coverage than the reporters' negative opinions on the police department's handling of the case. But every woman in town knew the dangers lurking in the darkness. Every woman who lived here knew the details of the crimes—what to look for and what to avoid.

She was one woman, alone in the city. And even though she was no slim, head-turning beauty, she wasn't so naive to think she couldn't become a victim, too. She fit the profile of the professional women the rapist targeted. She was successful and confident— when it came to her business, at any rate. Hope was smart enough to be on guard, especially at this time of night. But she couldn't very well surrender to the terror she faced as a single woman in this neighborhood. Her entire life's savings was tied up in this shop. Anything she could call her own was in that apartment upstairs.

Besides, she was experienced enough in life to know that danger could find a person anywhere—in the heart of the city, or on a dusty back road in the middle of nowhere. This building was her home and her livelihood, and no man—no threat—was going to frighten her into giving up everything she'd worked so hard for. She just had to be aware. She had to pay attention to the alerts and details the police had shared with the public.

Details.

Driven to another location...

Hope shifted the box of photos to one arm and closed the trunk as a shiver of awareness raised goose bumps across her skin. *That* was what she should have remembered about the white van that had cruised past her. She'd read a witness account in the paper with vague details about coming to inside a white van before being dumped in the alley across the street after her assault.

White van? A driver hiding his face on a cool autumn night?

There had to be hundreds of white vans in the city. Just because one had crept up on her bumper...twice...

And the man in black and white behind the wheel? Surely he wasn't... Hope's stomach knotted with fear. Surely she hadn't gotten a glimpse of the Rose Red Rapist himself.

En route to another abduction.

Returning from the scene of an assault.

"No. Surely not." No one had seen the serial rapist. One reason he'd never been arrested was that no victim had been able to identify him—no surviving victim. She hugged the box to her chest and tried to talk herself off the ledge of fearful possibility she was climbing on to. "He was just some jackass who was in a hurry."

A blur of white in Hope's peripheral vision drew her attention out to the street.

A white van moved with the late-night traffic past the entrance to the parking lot. *The* white van? Was the Rose Red Rapist on the prowl for his next victim?

Hope's breathing locked up the way it had at the church. She was squarely and completely trapped on that ledge. "That can't be him."

Cruising through *her* neighborhood? Had the driver followed her home? Was he hunting *her*?

Hope barely managed to save the box and its fragile contents from crashing to the asphalt. "You don't even know if it's him," she warned herself on a whisper. "It's just a white van. It's just some guy in a van. It's probably not even the same one."

Refusing to let her imagination turn her observation into a panic, she carefully set the box down on the trunk and took a couple of steps toward the street. Rusting wheel wells. Shiny silver bumper.

She glanced up into the cab. Dark stocking cap and...not a scarf.

A surgical mask.

Shadowed eyes met hers.

"Oh, my God."

Hope slipped her hand into her coat pocket to pull out her phone as the van suddenly picked up speed and headed toward the next intersection. She hurried out to the sidewalk to see which direction the vehicle would turn and punched in 911. The driver might not be the Rose Red Rapist, but it was definitely the same van that had nearly crowded her off the road tonight.

"Nine-eleven Dispatch," a succinct female voice answered. "What is the nature of your emergency?"

"I don't know if this is exactly an emergency, but I'm not sure who to report this to." Hope turned up the collar of her trench coat and huddled against the suddenly brisk chill in the autumn air. "I just saw a white van that matches the description the police gave in the paper about the vehicle the Rose Red Rapist drives. The man inside had his face covered."

"Are you in danger, ma'am?"

"I…" There were a few people hanging out down at the corner where the van was waiting for the light to change. A group of young women wandered out of the dance club. Was the driver watching them? Choosing one for his next victim? "I'm not. But someone else may be." Hope glanced around at the cars parked on the street, at the closed shops, at the deserted sidewalks here in the middle of the block. She was safe, wasn't she? The van turned right, slowly circling past the group of women waiting at the crosswalk. "I think you should send the police."

"Yes, ma'am. Where are you now?"

Hope relayed her location, refusing to take her eyes off the van until it disappeared from sight. A man wearing a surgical mask wasn't necessarily a threat. Maybe it was part of his work—such as an exterminator, or someone who worked with food might wear. Or maybe he was one of those people who was phobic about catching germs. Still…it just didn't feel right.

"We already have an officer in the area, ma'am," the dispatcher assured her. "I'll send him to your shop right now."

Good idea. Go back inside her shop. Lock the doors.

"Thank you."

Hope disconnected the call, waiting a few seconds longer until the young women changed their minds and went back into the club for more dancing. The breeze whipped loose a long tendril of hair that had been pinned up in a French roll all day. The long curl hooked inside the temple of her glasses and caught in her lashes, forcing her to squint until she pulled it free and tucked it back behind her ear. Good. The women were all safely inside. She'd be smart to do the same until the police arrived to take her statement.

"Staring into space like you always did."

Hope jumped inside her pumps and whirled around to see the gray-haired man standing behind her.

"I've been waitin' for you, girl."

"Damn it, Hank."

"Don't you get fresh with me, girl. I'm your father." Not anymore, he wasn't. And though he wasn't much taller than Hope, he could still point his finger and somehow manage to look down at her. "You watch your tongue. Here."

He held out a small box wrapped in brown paper and packing tape. Hope pulled her hands back to her stomach, instinctively retreating from his touch. "Go away."

"Hey, if you don't answer my phone calls, then I've got to come find you in person." His twangy, low-pitched drawl grated against her eardrums. His face was clean-shaven; his clothes were clean. But Hope could smell the booze on him. Or maybe those were the bad memories. What some people might describe as folksy charm, she knew to be a lie, a facade that hid the monster underneath.

"So it *was* you," she accused, referring to the countless unanswered calls and hang-ups she'd gotten on her phone today. "We have nothing to say."

She turned to the parking lot, but stopped after a few steps when she realized he was following. Apparently, changing phone numbers and ignoring his calls hadn't sent the message she wanted any more than moving away from the Ozarks when she was eighteen had. Getting rid of her father tonight would require one of those confrontations she hated.

Hope tugged the sleeves of her blouse and suit jacket over her wrists, and turned up the collar of her trench coat. "What are you doing in Kansas City?" As if she couldn't guess.

"Truck broke down. I need some cash to get parts to fix it."

"How did you get to K.C. if your truck's broken?" She followed his glance over his shoulder to see the a middle-aged woman with brassy hair tapping her dark red nails against the steering wheel of the compact car she sat in. "Friend of yours?"

The woman waved when he winked a smoky gray eye, one of the few traits Hope had inherited from him. "Don't you be rude, girl. I've been seeing Nelda for a couple of weeks now. She was nice enough to drive me up to the city from Wentworth. We're staying with a cousin of hers here in town. Oh, I'll be owin' her for gas, too."

"Then get a job."

He folded his stout arms over his belly, reminding her of the wrapped package he'd brought her. He nodded toward the front of her shop. "Why don't you give me one? You seem to be doin' well enough."

"I'm not hiring you."

"I could do odd jobs around the place for you. Sweep up at night. Fix the plumbing and electrical. Help haul all that stuff inside." He'd been watching her unload her car? Hope started to shake, although she wasn't sure if it was anger at his lazy rudeness, just sitting there and watching her work, or fear that he'd been spying on her, lying in wait, and she hadn't noticed—hadn't even suspected—that heated her blood. "You need a man around the place."

She didn't need *him*. Hope swallowed her emotions and kept her voice calm. "I have someone who takes care of those jobs. I have nothing for you." And that's when she saw the canceled stamps above her name on the package. It wasn't a gift he'd brought to try and buy his way back into her life. "You picked up my mail?"

"Just this." This time, she took the parcel when he held it out to her. "It wouldn't fit through the mail slot and was sitting outside your door. Didn't want some-one to take it." Unfortunately, someone *had* taken it.

She studied the box for a moment, idly noting the lack of a return address, wondering at the plain brown wrapping when everything she ordered for her store came through a professional delivery service. What-ever was inside didn't weigh much, but the contents seemed to shift each time she turned the box. She hoped it hadn't come from her brother, who was currently sta-tioned in the Middle East, because she suspected that whatever was inside had broken. "You do know it's a federal offense to take someone's mail? I have every right to call the police."

That made his silver brows bristle. "I'm your father. I was doing you a favor."

Hope shook her head. "It's not worth what you're asking me for. There's a reason I don't answer the phone when you call. And it's not because I want to see you in person, instead. You're not a part of my life anymore. Not legally, and certainly not emotionally."

"That's a lie, girl. I know how that heart of yours works. I know you want to be a part of something." He stepped closer and Hope flinched. His eyes sparkled with satisfaction. He probably knew he'd finally pushed the right button to get around her resolve. His gaze darted to the bare fingers on her left hand. "I know you ain't got a man in your life."

"And you think being a family with you and—" she gestured to the car at the curb "—Nelda is some kind of consolation prize? No, thanks."

Ending the late-night conversation, Hope turned away. But five strong fingers clamped down like a vise on her arm. She instantly tugged at his grip, but he jerked her shoulder back into his chest and whispered beside her ear, "We're family. I paid my debt for what I did. How many ways can I say I'm sorry?"

Her pulse throbbed beneath the scars at her wrist and neck and suddenly she was ten again. Suddenly she felt weak. Trapped. Afraid. "Hank, I—"

"Hank!" A car horn honked at the same time a siren whooped through one warning cycle. Flashing lights reflected in Hope's glasses and bounced off the windows of her shop as a black-and-white pickup truck screeched to a stop in the parking lot entrance behind them.

Hank Lockhart released his daughter's arm and shushed the brassy-haired woman who'd sounded the alarm. Hope clutched the package in her hand and rubbed at the bruised skin above her elbow.

She, too, backed off a step when she heard the fierce barking coming from the cage in the backseat of the truck. She held her breath as a wheaten-haired cop in a black uniform and KCPD ball cap jumped out of the hastily parked truck and circled around the front. She recognized the blue eyes and rugged features and felt an embarrassed awareness choke her throat. *This* was the cop KCPD had sent? Could her night get any worse?

Pike Taylor rested his hand on the gun at his waist as his broad shoulders came up behind her father and dwarfed him. "Is everything all right, Miss Lockhart?"

Chapter Two

Why did that woman jump every time he spoke to her?

Edison "Pike" Taylor bit down on the urge to curse and concentrated on the wiry older man who'd put his hands on Hope Lockhart. With his canine partner, Hans, loudly making it known that Pike had backup— in case six feet four inches of armed cop wasn't intimidating enough—he subtly maneuvered around the gray-haired coot who smelled as if he'd just walked out of a bar. Despite a nonchalant adjustment to the bill of his KCPD ball cap, Pike turned his shoulder into the space between Hope and her assailant, blocking any chance of the man reaching for her again.

Damn it. She drifted back another step, as if she was just as afraid of him as she was this guy. He and Hans had been patrolling this neighborhood for months now. And, as members of KCPD's Rose Red Rapist task force, they had answered every call to the scene of a female assault victim in the area, including one this past summer to the flower shop across the street that Hope's friend Robin Carter—well, Robin Lonergan now that she'd recently married—owned.

Up until that night, Hope Lockhart had been this prim, uptight shop owner—a stereotyped old maid who wore glasses, buttoned-up suits and her hair in a bun. She'd said barely more than "Hello, Officer" to him whenever they ran into each other on the street. She was either too busy, too snooty or too disinterested to make friendly conversation with him, despite his best efforts. It had become a challenge of sorts every day or night he worked for Pike to walk Hans by her storefront and wave or tip his hat to her through the display windows to see her sputter or blush or quickly turn away.

But on the night of the flower shop attack, when Hope had come over to check on the well-being of her friend Robin, and Robin's infant daughter, he'd suddenly seen her in a whole new light.

Hope Lockhart wasn't a snob at all. She was shy—a woman on the quiet side—maybe about as awkward making conversation with him as he'd been trying to tease and get a rise out of her. Hope Lockhart was guarded, a little mysterious, even. She was pretty, too. Not in a knock-your-socks-off kind of way. But if a man looked—and he'd been doing more looking than he should have that night—he'd notice there was more to Hope than a tight bun and those boring suits she wore like some kind of uniform.

That night she'd worn the same trench coat she had on now, hastily tied over a nightgown, showing a V of creamy skin that dropped down between some seriously generous breasts. Without the pins and barrettes, long, curly hair tumbled over her shoulders in sexy, toffee-colored waves. He'd noticed her eyes behind those skinny glasses that night, too. They were big and gray and deep like a placid fishing lake early in the morning before any boats or lines had disturbed the surface. But she'd about bolted from the room and gone all shades of pale when he'd tried to talk to her. Kind of hard on a man's ego.

Shyness didn't explain why she didn't like him much. But with her unwillingness to get better acquainted, he had no idea why. An aversion to cops? Was she intimidated by big men? Had he said something to offend her? Hope's reaction to him that night—and every other time he and Hans had crossed her path since—read fear to him. And that kind of fear—when he was damn sure he was one of the good guys—rubbed him the wrong way.

Pike glanced down over the jut of his shoulder to see Hope massaging the arm this man had grabbed. "Are you hurt, ma'am?"

That gray gaze darted up to meet his for a split second before dropping down to the pavement. "I'm okay."

Anything creamy or sexy or pretty was locked up tight beneath the buttoned-up coat and tightly pinned hair she wore tonight. Pike discovered that that bothered him, too. Why would a woman go to so much effort to hide what were potentially the prettiest things about her?

Hiding? Afraid?

Ah, hell. Why hadn't he fit the puzzle pieces together sooner? If Hope's covered-up appearance and skittish behavior didn't speak to some history of abuse, Pike didn't know what did.

Pike focused squarely on the man in front of him, even though he spoke to Hope. "Do you want him to stay?"

"We were just having a conversation, Officer, um…" The older man squinted the name on Pike's shirt into focus. "Taylor. I'm Hank Lockhart—Henry Lockhart the first." He extended a hand that Pike ignored. "I'm

Hope's daddy. I happened to be in town and thought I'd drop by and have a visit."

Her *daddy?* Paying a surprise visit after midnight?

"Hank?" A blonde woman, wearing a top that was too tight and skimpy for her age and the autumn weather, climbed out from behind the wheel of a parked Toyota. "Is everything all right? You said this would only take a minute. You've kept me waiting for more than an hour."

"Not now, Nelda." Hank waved off the woman, who'd tried to signal Pike's arrival when he pulled up.

"You didn't say she was friends with the cops. You said this was going to be easy—"

Hank swung around, pointing a bony finger at the woman. "Get back in the car."

With an annoyed huff, the woman tossed back her overbleached hair and slid behind the wheel.

Friends with the cops.

Pike slipped another peek at the woman cradling a small package in her hand and warily keeping an eye on everyone involved in this late-night tête-à-tête, including him. Hope didn't seem any more open to the idea of becoming friends now than she'd been during the other brief encounters they'd shared. And though he wished he knew what he'd done to earn such a cool reception from the bridal shop owner, Pike knew he didn't have to be liked by all the residents he'd sworn to protect and serve—he just had to protect and serve them.

"Did you want to press charges against him, ma'am?" Pike asked.

"Charges?" both Lockharts answered in unison.

But while Hope didn't seem to know how to answer the question, Hank had no trouble arguing his innocence in the matter. "Charge me with what? We were having a family discussion. A private one, I might add. I don't know where you came from or why you're here. But I haven't done anything wrong."

"Hope?" Pike prodded, willing her to snap out of her meek silence. He'd come here, looking for a suspicious white van, and he'd shown up right in the middle of some kind of domestic dispute. He could arrest this guy and make him go away for the night, but not for any longer if she refused to speak up. Pike hooked his thumbs into the top of his utility belt and waited for an answer. "What do you want me to do?"

Nelda honked the horn again and Hank swore beneath his breath.

To Pike's surprise, he heard a soft voice behind him. "My father was just leaving."

So the old man hadn't completely knocked the spirit out of her.

"We're not finished, girl," Hank dared to argue. When he turned that bony finger on Hope and took a step toward her, Pike quickly shifted to block his path. "About that job we were discussing—"

"I said he was leaving."

The rising confidence in Hope's tone made it that much easier to back her up—and made it clear that in this situation, at least, she'd appreciate a little help from him. Pike nodded toward the irritated blonde. "I wouldn't want to keep you, Mr. Lockhart."

The grizzled older man sized up Pike with one contemptuous glance, then angled his head to make a final plea to his daughter. "Don't you do this to me. You can't punish me forever. You know I need—"

"I suppose it's about time to walk my dog." Pike pulled out his black, reinforced leather gloves and nodded to the muscular German shepherd fogging up the rear window of his departmental vehicle, intently watching Pike's every move. Right on cue, the dog started barking again. "Hans has been cooped up inside my truck for a long time tonight."

He watched the color bleed from Hank Lockhart's cheeks, making the broken capillaries in his alcoholic's nose stand out in redder, sharper detail. That's what he figured. Pike's canine partner had a knack for convincing people to do exactly what Pike asked.

"I get your message loud and clear." Offering a placating hand that sported half a dozen homemade tattoos that indicated the man had done some jail time, Hank Lockhart finally retreated. "I'll talk to you later."

A soft trace of vanilla joined the damp scent of dying leaves on the late-night breeze as Hope stepped onto the sidewalk beside Pike to watch Hank and his lady friend drive off down the street. The sounds of a heated argument leaked through the open car windows and faded as the car turned the corner and vanished into the night.

Pike stuffed his gloves back into his pocket. "He's hurt you before, hasn't he?"

Hope's breathy sigh was confirmation enough. So maybe he'd been a little blunt with his speculation. Knowing she'd grown up with an abusive man went a long way toward explaining her ready distrust of him. And made him more determined than ever to prove that he wasn't the bad guy here.

A long twist of honey-brown hair had freed itself from the severe confinement of the clip at the back of her head and lifted like a feathery banner in the breeze. As she captured the wayward curl and tucked it behind her ear, Pike realized that that was where the sweet scent from a moment ago had come from. Once again, he wondered why Hope Lockhart would hide something so feminine and pretty as that glorious hair from the world.

Either unaware of or uninterested in the stirrings of awareness she sparked inside him, Hope turned away to the parking lot, dismissing him. "Good night, Officer Taylor."

Pike got the brush-off message but followed her, anyway. "Do you have a restraining order against him?"

She set aside a small package on the rear fender of her car and reached for a bigger, heavier box. "I haven't seen him for a couple of years. He doesn't even live in Kansas City."

"He's here now. I'd consider filing for one." Pike nudged her aside and picked up the box for her. "Where to?"

Her mouth opened to voice a protest, but once she understood he wasn't leaving her here alone at this time of night, she pointed to the side entrance of her shop. "Thank you."

"Miss Lockhart—Hope—is it okay if I call you that?" After a momentary hesitation, she nodded and opened the door for him. "You want to tell me about that 911 call?"

She held open the interior door, as well. "It had nothing to do with my father, Officer Taylor."

"Pike."

"Pike," she repeated, then paused, knotting the smooth skin above the nosepiece of her glasses. "What kind of name is Pike?"

He grinned, seeing the first opportunity for a normal, friendly conversation between them. "There's a story behind it. Taylor is my adoptive parents' name. But I was born Edison Pike."

No comment. But the curiosity was still there.

So he forged ahead. "Like Thomas Edison. I think my grandmother who raised me was hoping for an inventor—someone brainier than I turned out to be. And for a while, I did think about going into veterinary medicine. But what can I say? I come from a family of cops and firefighters. I always liked the action more than the books. But I kept the nickname as a way of honoring the woman who took care of me for the first few years of my life."

She tilted her eyes up to his, flashing him a look that said his words didn't make sense, before she led him through her shop to the back room. "Your grandmother raised you—but you're adopted?"

Well, at least he knew she'd been listening. Pike ignored the gowns, mannequins and fancy accessories surrounding him and focused in on the curly lock bouncing against Hope's neck as she walked. "Gran died when I was ten. I went into foster care, where I met my mom and dad and my three brothers. They're adopted, too. Alex is the oldest. Then there's me, Matthew and Mark."

Hope turned on the light and hugged the door frame to stay out of his way as he carried the box into the storage room. He set the box of picture frames and photo albums down on the shelf she indicated. "There was no other family to take me when Gran got sick. I lucked out, though. My mom, Meghan, had been a foster child in the same house when she was younger, and she liked to come back and help out whenever she could. She brought me my first dog—a smaller, mutt version of Hans—that she'd rescued from a fire. I named her Crispy. I think Mom kind of adopted us even before she married Gideon Taylor."

Pike paused when he realized he was rambling to

fill up the silence. He reached over Hope's shoulder to turn off the light switch and watched her scuttle out of the room, leaving a trail of vanilla deliciousness in her wake. Hmm. Maybe the KCPD brass had made a mistake in selecting him and Hans to do frontline PR and security work between the task force and the community. Apparently, his presence was more unsettling than reassuring—at least with this particular community member.

Protect and serve. Forget the sweet fragrance and tempting lock of hair. He just had to earn Hope's trust and keep her safe. She didn't have to like him.

Inhaling a deep, resigning breath, Pike followed Hope out to the counter at the center of the shop. "I'm doing all the talking. If you don't say something soon, I'll never shut up."

Was that…? No. A smile?

"I don't mind. I like to listen."

Some unknown weight lifted off his chest and Pike grinned right back. He'd almost made her laugh.

But just as soon as it had softened her mouth, Hope's smile disappeared. She pulled her purse from beneath the counter and looped the strap over her shoulder. "I was a foster kid, too. My mother passed when my brother was born. And Hank wasn't… He couldn't handle her death and we… Harry—my brother—is just a year younger. When I aged out of the system, I filed for guardianship and we moved to Kansas City. I went to school and Harry enlisted in the Marines."

"Sounds a lot like my mom's story."

Ah, hell. Wrong thing to say. Telling a young woman she reminded him of his mother—no matter how much he loved that mother—wasn't the smoothest line a man could use.

Just as he thought he was getting somewhere with Hope, her body language became all stern business again, and she spun toward the parking lot exit. "I called because there was a van following me home from the wedding I worked today. At least, I thought it might be. When I saw it drive past my shop several minutes later, I realized it matches the description of the van your task force may be looking for."

Pike shook his head at the abrupt change in topic. But then the import of what she was saying hit and he hurried after her to catch her before she reached the door. He turned in front of her, blocking her path. "This van was following you?"

She tipped her head back, adjusting her glasses at her temple to look him in the eye even though she was sliding back a step. "I don't know that he was intentionally following *me*. But he was driving behind me, maybe a little closer than I'd like, on the street. When I saw him drive by again and circle the block, that's when I called KCPD."

This was exactly the type of lead the task force had been looking for. And he'd been worried about making nice with her? "Did you get a license plate? A description of the driver?"

She shook her head. "I can't tell you much. He was dressed in black. Wore a stocking cap pulled down over his forehead and…"

"And what?"

Her shoulders lifted as though she doubted what she'd seen. "At first I thought he was wearing a white scarf around his neck. But I got a closer look the second time he drove by. He had on a surgeon's mask." She raised her hand to her face to indicate how little she'd been able to see. "It covered his nose, mouth and chin."

Wait a minute. Pike propped his hands on his belt, tuning in to the details beyond her description of the driver. "The second time?"

She nodded. "He circled the block and came back by the shop."

"Did he see you? Do you think he was looking for you?"

"I don't know. I know we made eye contact, but then he sped off and my father showed up and…" She shrugged again. "Sorry I can't tell you more. But I can give a pretty accurate description of the van if that helps."

"We'll take whatever help we can get if it leads us to our rapist." Pike hesitated a moment before stepping aside and following her into the vestibule and waiting for her to lock the shop door. He guessed the other interior door, built of antique walnut and bolted tight, led upstairs to the apartment above the shop. Had she carried in all those other boxes, packed with the similar white netting and tissue paper tonight? By herself? After midnight?

With a serial rapist at large in the city?

How many other nights had she worked this late and come home alone? Even if the guy in the van wasn't the Rose Red Rapist, and her father hadn't been on-site to bully her, she'd been at risk.

Swallowing the acrid taste that suspicion left in his throat, Pike gave one last glance at the racks of fancy dresses and froufrouy displays that marked her bridal shop as foreign territory. He was too big, too male, too comfortable in his black uniform to ever fit in with all the lace and glitz and monkey suits there. Maybe that's why she'd barely spoken a dozen words to him over the past few months. They had next to nothing in common.

But ignoring the extra security he provided this neighborhood wasn't an option. Not anymore. Hope Lockhart needed to accept somebody's help in making her habits smarter and safer.

"How often do you come home late like this?" he asked, holding the outside door open for her.

"Once or twice a month," she answered, walking to the trunk of her car. "Depending on how elaborate the wedding is and how late the ceremony or reception runs."

Pike reached behind the badge on his belt to pull out a KCPD business card with his contact information on it. "Next time you've got a car full of stuff to unload by yourself late at night, you call me."

"I'm perfectly capable of—"

"I'm not talking muscle." The breeze lifted the distracting swirl of caramel hair again and Pike was reaching for it before he'd even thought the impulse through. He caught the silky twist and wound it around his fingertip, watching twin dots of color warm her cheeks as he tucked it behind her ear. Yeah, maybe his hand lingered a little longer than it should have, but those curls were just as soft as they looked. "I'm talking company. You shouldn't be alone on the streets or in this parking lot after dark. It'd make my job a lot easier if I knew I didn't have to worry about one of the locals getting herself into trouble with a serial rapist—or a long-lost father."

"I'll try not to be a bother." She pressed her hand against her ear and the nape of her neck, as though checking to see if the wayward strand he'd touched was still there. Her eyes darkened and she turned away, acting as if his curious touch had somehow upset her.

"That's not what I meant."

She hurried to retrieve the small parcel still sitting there, never giving him a chance to apologize.

"I know what you..." The box toppled off the trunk of her car before her fingers ever touched it. It landed flat on the ground, came to a complete rest, then wobbled on the asphalt. The thing rocked back and forth, moving several inches, as though it had sprouted feet and was slinking away. "That's weird."

When she went to pick it up, Pike latched onto her arm and pulled her back. "Hold on. Is that box from the wedding?"

"No." She quickly moved away, hugging an arm around her waist and clutching her collar together at the neck. "My father had it when I came home."

Pike let her go and squatted down to get a closer look at the package. Loosely taped. Plain brown wrapping. Moving away like a drunken snail. Something was wrong here. "Gift from your dad?"

"He handed it to me. Said he picked it up outside my door. I'm not sure where it came from."

Pike read Hope's name and this address scribbled directly onto the brown paper. "You got any friends who are into practical jokes? Maybe it's full of Mexican jumping beans."

But Hope wasn't laughing. "I thought it might be from my brother overseas. He's in the Marines. But there's no APO address, country of origin or customs label, either."

"There's no cancelation stamp, period. This didn't come through the mail. If your dad didn't bring it, then someone left it here." Pulling his gloves from his hip pocket, Pike rose to his feet. "Let me get Hans out to check it before you open it."

"That's not necessary. I..."

But Pike was already heading to his truck. He pulled Hans's leash from the front seat before opening the back door. "Hey, big guy. Want to go to work?"

The familiar whines of anticipation were as clear as a verbal yes. Pike rubbed his hands around the German shepherd's jowls and neck, reinforcing their bond and cueing his intention before he clipped the work leash to the harness between Hans's shoulders. Pike rotated the dog's collar so his brass badge hung in front of his deep chest. Then he patted the tan fur twice and issued the command to exit the truck.

Jogging at a pace that gave Hans a chance to stretch his muscles, Pike took him in a circle around the perimeter of the parking lot before he tugged on the lead and slowed the dog to put his sensitive black nose to work. "Find it, boy. *Such!*"

Working in methodical steps along the building's south brick wall and around Hope's car, Pike let Hans sniff the ground and vehicle. This was a game for the dog. In addition to his security work, he'd been trained to search for certain particular scents, and once he found one and sat to indicate his discovery, he'd be rewarded with a game of tug-of-war with his favorite toy. If Pike led him straight to the box, Hans might not identify it as anything suspicious because he hadn't had the chance to track the scent first.

"There he goes." Hans's rudderlike tail wagged with excitement as he zeroed in on the trunk of the car. His breathing quickened and his nose stayed down as he picked up the trail of the mysterious package. "Find, it, Hansie," Pike encouraged, repeating the command in German. *"Such!"*

His black nose hovered over the package, touched the ground beside it. He whined at a high pitch, then jumped back as the package moved again. Hans was panting heavily now, more worked up with excitement than with the duration of the search.

"What is it, boy?" The dog lifted his dark brown eyes to Pike and sat. "He's not hitting on it like he does when there are drugs or explosives inside." The dog's high-pitched squeal indicated a degree of discomfort or uncertainty. "This is something different. I don't think it's anything dangerous or he'd let us know, but I'm damn curious to open it."

After tossing Hans his toy, and giving him a few seconds of play time to reward him for completing his job, Pike pulled his utility knife from his belt and flipped it open. "I'm going to go ahead and open it. Unless you want to?"

With a cautious hand, Pike slit open the packing tape and peeled off the outer wrapping. As he set the paper aside, he turned his ear to a clicking noise coming from the tottering box. He leaned closer. Not clicking. Chattering. Shuffling, maybe. Oh, man. Was there something alive in there? Forgetting caution and feeling pity for whatever poor creature had been trapped inside, he sliced through the cardboard and pulled open the flap.

"Whoa." Pike landed on his backside as he jerked away from the bugs tumbling out through the opening in the box. Hans barked at Pike's surprise as the insects poured out, scurrying across the asphalt, seeking their freedom. Dozens of them. Hundreds, maybe. Cockroaches. Crickets. Centipedes. Creepies and crawlies he couldn't identify. "What sick son of a…?"

He scrambled to his feet and backed toward Hope, positioning himself between her and the swarm of shock and terror. "Don't come over here. You don't need to see this… Hope?" Pike spun around, desperate for a glimpse of prim-looking glasses and tied-up hair. "Hope!"

She was gone.

Chapter Three

"Hope? Hope!"

"Get back here, girl! You runnin' from me?"

Hope bolted the door behind her and scrambled up the stairs, desperate to put some distance between her and that huge, horrible monster.

The bugs were gross, a sick joke—maybe even from her dad. Probably meant to scare her into thinking she needed a man here. Maybe he'd even hoped she'd open the box inside her shop or apartment and then she'd hire him to exterminate every last one of them. Never. A bug she could step on.

But the dog…

"Hope?" The pounding on the door pushed her across the landing, past the double door leading to a loft storage area and straight to the restored antique door to her apartment. She dropped her keys when a thundering bark joined the pounding. "Are you in there? Are you okay?"

Knowing she was acting on blind panic, but feeling just as helpless to stop it, she scooped up the fallen keys and unlocked the door.

"Hope? Answer me!" Wood splintered around the

lock below as she pushed open the door and ran straight to her kitchen. "Go, boy! *Voran!* Hope?"

She yelped when she heard the galloping up the stairs, the long legs running her down. The rapid drumbeat filled up her ears and she could barely catch her breath. She swiped away the foolish tears that stung her eyes and reached for the biggest weapon she could find.

Pulling a carving knife from the butcher block on the counter, Hope swung around into the open dining and living area to meet the beast at her front door. A man in black filled up the opening, but he was just the imposing backdrop to the real threat.

Gripping the knife in both hands, Hope prepared to defend herself. Far better than she had done twenty years ago. This time, she was no little girl. This time, she wasn't weak from starvation. This time, she was armed.

She heard the growl. Saw the rush of movement. Screamed.

"Hans! *Platz!*"

The charging dog halted as if he'd jerked to the end of an invisible chain and plopped back onto his haunches. He slowly walked his feet forward until he was lying down beside the black military-grade boots of the man in the doorway. Hope didn't believe that relaxed posture for a moment. The dog was breathing just as hard as she was, and those big, midnight-brown eyes still had her in his sights.

"Miss Lockhart?" The man raised one hand in a placating motion, then stooped down to clip a leash to the harness the dog wore. He dropped his voice to a deep, husky pitch. "Hope?"

Something short-circuited in her brain, cutting off the instinctive fight-or-flight response long enough for her to see what was really happening here. Pushing the falling hair off her face, still breathing deeply and erratically, still holding the knife, Hope blinked Edison Pike Taylor into focus. Clear blue eyes in a rugged, masculine face. Broad shoulders. Black ball cap. KCPD embroidered on the shirt that stretched over a black turtleneck and protective vest. A badge and gun on his belt.

Not her father. Not the damned babysitters. *"Get her!"*

Hope cringed and looked away from the ugly nightmare that tried to surface.

Pike Taylor slowly straightened, filling up the doorway again. "Why did you run? I turned around and you were gone. I thought you'd been abducted or something— that maybe your dad had come back or…" He took a step toward her and she lifted the knife, gripping it between both hands. He stopped, put up his leather-gloved hand again and drilled her with those startling blue eyes. "Don't be afraid of me."

The sharp words, more command than request, pierced the fog of fear that lingered in her brain. "I…I'm not. I don't think I am."

"Could have fooled me." His gaze dropped briefly to the knife she still wielded, and she suddenly realized that with a gun and a guard dog and the sheer size and strength he had over her, she hadn't stood much chance of defending herself, anyway. But he still didn't make another move toward her. "Did you see something out there? That van? Was it the bugs? Trust me, they've scattered."

"They're not especially pleasant, but—"

"Is it me?"

She was the target of Pike Taylor's piercing blue eyes again. "Not exactly."

She couldn't handle the intensity there—the suspicion? The anger? Hope blinked. She blinked again, trying to understand exactly what was happening here. Damn, he was big—more man than had ever been in her apartment before. He'd come by her shop nearly every day for months now—had always tipped his hat and said hello or winked as if they were some kind of friends. And now he was in her apartment, shrinking the wide-open space down to the few feet that separated them.

Why had he touched her hair tonight? And why had she…? Her heart had never raced like that before—not with anything except fear. Why had his fingers tangling into her wayward hair felt like a caress? As if she had the experience to recognize a man's gentle caress.

Hope shook her head, dispelling the unfamiliar imprint of a man's warm hand brushing across her cheek and ear. Blue eyes and distracting touches didn't matter. She couldn't afford to take her gaze off the black and tan dog. She could smell him now—the heat of his panting breath, the outdoor scents that clung to his thick fur. Hope finally lowered the knife, but only to slide her fingers beneath the sleeves on her right arm and rub at her wrist. The ridges and dots had softened and faded over the years, but she could feel the pain and itch of every scar as if they were new.

"Is it Hans?" At this hushed volume, Pike's deep voice danced along her fried nerves like a soothing balm.

As embarrassing as her phobia might be to admit, her behavior put her past the point of lying or making a joke about it. Hope nodded. "I'm sorry. I guess I had a panic attack."

"You think?"

"I haven't had one for a long time. I usually can control it. But with the running and…and he was tracking so hard, so relentlessly. He's so strong—all muscle, isn't he?" She pushed her glasses into place at her temple, then found her fingers sliding beneath the collar of her blouse and loose hair to touch the scar there. She'd lost her big hair clip somewhere, and had probably left a trail of bobby pins on the stairs. Her hair was most likely sticking out in all directions, looking as wild as the pulse beat at the side of her neck felt. "I'm sure it seems irrational to you. I know he's specially trained, he's a member of the police force, and that he helps—"

"He's not going to hurt you."

"You don't know that." She blinked away flashback images of tearing flesh and searing pain. Of a gunshot that jerked through her even now. The final tragedy of two desperate children's struggle for survival.

"Stay with me, Hope." Pike stepped forward and Hope retreated.

"I am." She managed to keep the knife pointed to the floor, although she couldn't seem to ignore the phantom throb beneath the scars on her wrist. She pulled up a coat sleeve, a jacket sleeve and unbuttoned the cuff of her blouse to massage the skin there. "I will."

Tall, Blond and Rugged was moving closer again. Hope focused on the black button at the center of Pike's shirt. She could still hear the dog panting, but she could no longer see him past the width of those shoulders and chest.

"I trust Hans with my life. I trust he'll do whatever I say. He's trained to be an extension of me on the job,

not a rogue wild animal." Pike pulled off his cap and
rubbed at his short dark gold hair, leaving rumpled
spikes in its wake. He dropped his gaze to the leash in
his hand and followed it back to the dog lying in the
doorway behind him. The dog's black muzzle lifted
up and he tilted his head in some sort of anticipation.

Hope's fingers tightened around the knife handle.

But Pike raised his hand and the dog settled down
again, resting his head on his front legs. When Pike
faced Hope again, his narrowed, probing eyes looked
straight into hers. "I never had a chance at getting you
to trust me, did I. All these months I've been patrolling this neighborhood, I've been trying to get to know
you. Trying to find out if you were stuck-up or just unaware of my efforts."

Regret followed closely on the heels of her simmering panic, sapping the remainder of Hope's strength. It
was a shy person's worst nightmare to have her quiet
moods and awkward social skills mistaken for arro-
gance or indifference. It compounded her frustration
to discover that the time she needed to process her
thoughts, emotions and reactions could be interpreted
as a lack of caring. It hurt to know that the fight it took
to assert herself sometimes came off as disdain.

"I've even been a little ornery about it," Pike went
on. "Making up excuses to come by your shop, demanding that you give me your trust and respect. But you
were never going to give me a real chance."

"I'm not stuck-up," she whispered, mindlessly massaging the scars again.

"No. You're terrified. Doesn't make me feel like
much of a cop—or much of a man—to see you look at
me like that. I'd like to fix your perception of Hans and
me." He reached out, and for a moment, she thought

he intended to disarm her. Instead, he reached past the knife and slowly closed his fingers around her wrist, brushing the warm pad of his thumb across the pale web of scars there. "What happened to you?"

"I…" Gentle though his inquisitive touch might be, Hope jerked her arm away and quickly pulled down her sleeves. What did she tell him? Long version? Short version? Was there any version that didn't make her sound sad or eccentric or worth anything more than his pity?

Hans raised his head and woofed a split second before Pike turned his head and Hope heard a whisper of sound from the foot of the stairs. The outside door opened.

No version.

She clutched the knife in both hands again. There were knocks at both the shop and stairwell doors.

"Taylor!" a man shouted from the vestibule downstairs. "Pike! You here?"

"We're not done with this conversation." Pike adjusted his ball cap on his head and turned to the door. "I'm here!" he shouted. "Hans. *Fuss!*" The dog jumped to his feet and fell into step beside him. "Detective Montgomery? Nick? What are you doing here?"

Hope followed them out the door to see man and dog jog around the landing and down to the entryway below.

She heard a second man's voice now. "We saw your rig out front. Thought maybe you knew something we didn't."

"Knew something about what?" Pike asked.

Hope crept to the top of the stairs behind him. "He took someone else, didn't he? That's why he was here."

"The Rose Red Rapist?" At the foot of the stairs, Pike stood taller than either of the two men, one in a gray wool suit and tie, the other wearing jeans and a black leather jacket. The badges they wore identified them as cops, too.

Hope sank onto the top step, still holding the knife. "That was his van I saw, wasn't it? That was *him*."

The shorter of the two detectives pulled back the front of his leather jacket and reached for his gun, his gaze zeroing in on Hope—or, more specifically, on the carving knife she still held in her fist. "Ma'am? I need you to put that down."

Hope's breath locked up in her chest and she instinctively recoiled.

Pike put up a hand and warned the dark-haired detective not to unholster his weapon. "It's okay, Nick. She's a witness, not a threat. I…" His head tipped down toward Hans. "We…scared her."

The air gradually eased from her lungs at Pike's politely vague explanation. She'd pulled a knife and freaked out on him, yet he was still kind enough to defend her. And although she appreciated having that blockade of Pike Taylor's shoulders between her and the two plainclothes detectives, Hope wisely set the knife down on the floor beside her. She spotted two bobby pins on the next step down and remembered that she probably looked as if she'd been fighting something more than her own fears tonight.

The red-haired detective who seemed to be in charge slid his gaze up to her, too, assessing her unkempt appearance and dismissing her before giving a concise, emotionless report to Pike. "We've got a body dump around the corner in the alley. Red rose inside her coat."

Body dump? That meant the victim was dead, didn't it? Raped *and* murdered. Hope's audible gasp echoed through the walnut banister and across the crisply painted white landing. The dog's ear pricked to attention, but none of the men seemed to notice. Hope pressed her fingers to her lips and whispered, "Oh, God. She was inside there, wasn't she? She was in that van."

The red-haired detective heard her hushed voice and looked up the stairs. "A LaDonna Chambers. Do you know her?"

"LaDonna?" For a moment, the detective's hard eyes swam out of focus. But she blinked away the emotions that made her light-headed and nodded, picturing the friendly acquaintance she'd seen just yesterday morning. "Not well. She's interning at a law office on the next street over. I've waited in line with her at the coffee shop several times."

The detective in the suit jotted something into his notebook before tucking it inside his jacket pocket and turning his attention back to Pike. "Some college kids who'd been at Harpo's Dance Club found her. That's not the call you're answering?"

Pike shook his head. "Miss Lockhart called in that she'd seen a suspicious white van on her way home tonight. I came to take her statement."

"She saw the van?" The redhead pulled back the front of his jacket and splayed his hands at either side of his waist. "*His* van?"

Pike answered. "Could be, sir. She gave me a detailed description, but no plate number."

The dark-haired detective looked agitated. "When? Did she see our guy? Can she ID the driver? Is that what spooked her?"

Clearly, the two detectives suspected there was more to her story than a helpful citizen's phone call. But Pike didn't mention her father, the sick present she'd gotten or her off-the-charts paranoid reaction to his efforts to help her. Thankfully, neither detective had questioned her erratic behavior, either. Until now.

They had bigger problems than hers tonight.

"I'm Detective Spencer Montgomery, KCPD task force, ma'am. This is my partner, Detective Nick Fensom. We work with Officer Taylor here." Detective Montgomery flashed his badge and looked over Pike's shoulder, right at her. Somehow the intensity of that slate-colored gaze was even more unsettling than the threat of Detective Fensom's pulling his gun had been. "We need to talk to you."

"WELL, THAT WAS a lousy plan. Do you think she recognized you?"

"I don't know." He breezed past the woman in the negligee and robe and headed straight for the bathroom.

"You don't know?" She followed him in. "You already made one mistake tonight. I don't think we can afford another."

He unhooked his belt and slung it at her feet. "We?"

She crossed her arms beneath her breasts, refusing to let the subject drop. "I did my part. LaDonna Chambers can never hurt you again. But you don't even know if this woman—"

"Shut up. I need to think." He opened the shower door and turned on the shower until the water ran blisteringly hot. He stepped underneath the spray, clothes and all. He braced his hands on the tile wall and bent his head. The water beat against his scalp, drowning out the sounds of her calling him all kinds of stupid for going to the bridal shop tonight. Finally, she got the hint and returned to his bedroom. He stood there for countless minutes, letting the hot water sluice through his hair and soak through his clothes while the trapped, steamy air opened the pores of his skin. He stood like that until most of the rage was purged from him.

Once the haze of emotion had cleared his brain and reason returned, he peeled off his sodden clothes and dumped them into the hamper beside the shower. Then he unwrapped a fresh bar of soap and started to wash, cleaning beneath every nail, massaging every hair follicle, rinsing his skin twice and then again.

When he was done, exhausted by the furious emotions and the long night, he pulled a clean towel from the linen closet and wrapped it around his waist. He pulled out a matching towel to wipe down the shower walls and glass door. Then, with a third towel, he dropped down to his hands and knees, sopping up the puddle of water beneath the hamper.

He hated that he'd have to do something about Hope. He knew most of the women he hunted by their face, their habits, their location. But he rarely knew their names until their pictures were splashed across the television screen or centered in a newspaper article. He knew Hope, liked her well enough, he supposed. She stirred nothing inside him—no desire, no rage—but now he could see he'd been wrong to think she was of no consequence.

Hope Lockhart ran a successful business. She was loved by clients and respected by leaders in Kansas City business and society. Who'd have thought she'd have the guts to look him in the eye and call the police?

He'd have to find out exactly what she knew about him, exactly what she'd seen. If he was lucky, she'd still be of no consequence. But if she was a threat to him...

The damp towels fisted in his hands and he felt the stirrings of that damned hunger stirring inside him again.

"I suppose you need me to take care of this problem, too?"

She was in the doorway again, sneaking up behind him, standing over him. With his nostrils flaring as he fought to maintain his composure, he slowly eased his grip on the towels and folded them neatly around the wet clothes he'd discarded. "I'll handle it. You were messy tonight."

"Me? You're the one who was careless. I told you it was too soon, but you wouldn't listen."

"Really? A gun? Do you know how long it took me to clean up the blood?" He laid the squared package of damp clothes and towels in the bottom of the hamper before turning to face her. "I had everything under control. She was mine to use however I wanted—until you interfered."

"Do you think she would have given you what you wanted?" He went to the sink to unwrap a fresh comb. Her reflection joined his in the mirror. "She woke up, called you by name when she recognized your voice. I had to silence her."

"I wasn't finished with her."

"Oh, you were finished." She laughed.

His comb clattered into the sink. "Shut up."

"I'm the voice of reason in your sad, secretive life. I'm the only one who has always been here for you. Without me, you'd be rotting in prison. I know the lie you live and I've loved you any—"

He spun around, clamping his hand around her throat and shoving her against the wall. "I said, shut. Up."

"You won't hurt me. I made you. You need me."

What he needed was to feel in control again. His fingers tightened for a few moments until he heard her choking gurgle. But, damn her, even as her face drained

of color, she barely even blinked at the dangerous tor-
ture he inflicted.

He popped his fingers open and released her. She
inhaled a calm, deep breath and smiled. "You see? You
know you can't hurt me, that I'm the only one who'll
always be here for you." She left the room to pour herself a drink. "Now. What are you going to do about
Hope Lockhart?"

Chapter Four

The whole elevator smelled of vanilla, reminding Pike of the decadent sugar cookies his grandma Martha baked for Christmas every year.

Crossing his arms over his chest, he looked down at the toffee-haired woman standing at his shoulder, resolutely watching each number light up as they rode from the garage level up to the third floor of Fourth Precinct headquarters. She'd tamed her hair back into a loose ponytail, but a handful of curls escaped to frame her weary eyes. "You don't have to do this, you know."

It was maybe the fifth or sixth effort he'd made at starting a conversation with Hope Lockhart since driving her to the station for an interview with Detectives Montgomery and Fensom. *"Get her downtown. Let's talk to her while the memories are fresh."*

If he hadn't scared the memories right out of her.

In the truck he'd gotten nothing more than a couple of nods and some wild-eyed glances back at the dog caged securely in the seat behind them. Maybe now, with Hans secured in his kennel downstairs, he hoped the skittish woman might relax a bit and they could share some normal, friendly conversation like the kind they'd started at her shop.

Well, he got conversation. But there wasn't much normal or friendly about a woman talking to a pair of steel doors instead of to him.

"I know. But I want to help. Too many people I know have been hurt by that man. I barely knew LaDonna, but it feels like I've lost another friend. She splurged on mochas every Friday, and she had this big smile. Tonight she looked like she was sleeping. Until the M.E. closed that zipper..." Pike watched the ripple of movement down her creamy throat as Hope swallowed. "She was in a bag. Like...like she was being discarded."

"You shouldn't have agreed to confirm her ID." Sure, the quick confirmation helped speed the investigation along, but very few people got to look at dead bodies outside of a funeral home. So how did he reassure her? How did he stop feeling so guilty about everything she'd been through tonight? "It's a good thing, actually—the bag, I mean. It protects the evidence as much as it honors the victim's dignity and keeps others from seeing what can sometimes be a pretty disturbing sight."

He almost startled when she suddenly tipped her head and looked up at him. Even her glasses couldn't diminish the impact of her gaze locking onto his. Her eyes were as warm with concern as they were cool in color. "Have you seen a lot of that? *Disturbing* things?"

Pike dropped his arms and reached out, feeling the need to offer some kind of comfort. But he wisely curled his fingers into a fist and kept it at his side. The last thing he wanted to do was to scare her into silence again.

"More than I want to." Yeah. There was a lot of pretty to discover about this woman if a man took the time to look. Maybe he was doing a little too much looking. Taking a cue from the champ, he turned and focused his gaze on the elevator panel. "But you learn to turn off your emotions and you just deal with the facts."

"How do you do that? Turn off your emotions, I mean." She was staring straight ahead again, too. "Maybe I live inside my head too much. But sometimes, I can't stop thinking about things. I wish I could just *do.* And not overthink the consequences or second-guess myself."

"What do you want to do?" He couldn't help himself. The woman was too much of an enigma to ignore.

She shook her head, stirring the curls down her back. She wasn't going to answer.

"Come on, now. You've just said as many words to me as you've said in the entire twelve months I've known you." He nudged his shoulder against hers. "Are you going to stop talking to me now?"

Her eyes darted up to his at the teasing request. And was that a smile? Victory. "You're awfully patient with me, Officer Taylor."

"Pike."

"More persistent than most men I know. Why do you keep trying?"

He liked a challenge? He was a sucker for a complex mystery like this woman? He just plain couldn't stand the irritation of having someone not like him or his dog? "I am determined that you're going to look at me and not think I'm the evil villain in the fairy tale of your life."

"The fairy tale?" The smile disappeared and she fixated on the K-9 Corps patch sewn onto the sleeve of his uniform. "Oh. My shop. Believe me, my life isn't a fairy tale, Offic…Pike." And then her gaze crept back to his.

"There's no Prince Charming. There's no fairy god-mother. I just try to make the magic happen for others."

"Why aren't you making it happen for yourself, Hope?" And then he did the dumbest thing he'd done all night long. He tunneled his fingers beneath the silky knot of her ponytail, stroked his thumb along the line of her jaw to her chin and tilted his face down toward hers. "Why don't you have the fairy tale?"

She shivered beneath his touch, making him feel like all kinds of ogre for holding on just a little tighter to prevent her from pulling away when he felt the tug against his fingertips. He knew better. He trained dogs for a living and was smart enough not to try to pet one until it was comfortable around him and some ground rules for expected behavior had been laid down be-tween them. But her pink tongue darted out nervously to moisten her lips and an unexpected anticipation pinged him right in the groin.

Here was a shy, secretive woman who bolted or blushed every time he came near—and he wanted to kiss her?

The elevator stopping wasn't the only thing that had him swaying on his feet.

The elevator doors opened to the bustle and noise of KCPD's early morning shift change…and two men wearing expensive business suits who stopped their re-spective pacing and phone call the moment they spot-ted their arrival.

"Hope?" Pike's hand fell away as the dark-haired man wearing charcoal gray pulled Hope off the eleva-tor and straight into a tight hug. "Thank God. Are you all right?"

"Hey." At her startled *oof,* Pike's instinct was to

step in and break it up. But her arms gradually settled around the man's waist.

Besides, when Pike tried to intervene with a hand on her shoulder, the guy with the tan suit and the phone stepped between them and flashed a business card. "I'm Adam Matuszak, Miss Lockhart's attorney. If she's going to be interviewed by the police, then I need to be present."

"Matuszak. Why do I know that name?"

Hope pulled away from the hug. "LaDonna worked for him."

The dark-haired man draped an arm around her shoulders and was already walking her away before she'd finished. He tipped his mouth close to Hope's ear to say something that made her nod. Stealing her away. Shutting her up. Warning her…about what?

"Miss Chambers was an intern at my office," the lawyer confirmed, interrupting Pike's silent observations. "I believe my building is on your patrol."

Pike nodded toward the man taking Hope away. "Who's he?"

"Brian Elliott." The tall blond attorney pocketed his phone and smoothed his lapels. "He owns my building—and several others on your beat. He's Miss Lockhart's business associate—and a good friend."

How good? Pike ignored the stirrings of something he wasn't ready to name and unbuttoned the pocket of his uniform shirt to stuff the business card inside. Seeing his shot at making inroads with Hope disappearing down the hallway, he retreated a step. "I'm not the cop interviewing her. I'm just a…friend who brought her in."

He was instantly dismissed as inconsequential. "Who do I need to speak to, then?"

With a reluctant nod, Pike led Matuszak past the sergeant's desk to point out Spencer Montgomery and Nick Fensom. The attorney immediately crossed through the maze of desks to introduce himself to the two detectives, then signaled to Hope and her *good* friend to join them.

Since the third floor of Fourth Precinct headquarters housed the detectives' bull pen, conference area and meeting rooms—Pike didn't have a desk here. But he did have a badge and access to the KCPD computers. While Hope and her well-pressed bookends settled in across from Detective Montgomery, Pike made himself at home at the sergeant's desk. He intended to find out a little more about Hope Lockhart.

Even if she wasn't going to tell him herself.

If HENRY LOCKHART Sr. was as much of a lowlife as his criminal record indicated, then it was no wonder that his daughter, Hope, would be afraid of him. He'd served a nickel at the state pen in Jefferson City for domestic assault, multiple DUI/suspended license violations and animal cruelty.

Was Hope the domestic assault? More than once? Had she been witness to repeated violence in her own home?

Pike scanned the prison record on the computer screen at the desk sergeant's counter where he stood before sliding a glance across the third-floor squad room. The morning shift was changing—detectives and uniforms were straightening their desks and signing out as the A shift reported in, poured coffees and made their way toward the conference room for morning roll call.

Still, with all the comings and goings in and out of the elevators and from cubicle to cubicle, he had no trouble spotting the woman sitting across from Spencer Montgomery at his desk. Hope Lockhart's ponytail flared loosely down her back, looking a shade richer than the camel-colored trench coat she wore and reminding him of a lion's mane. Nick Fensom stood at Detective Montgomery's shoulder while the two men who'd whisked her off the elevator flanked her.

And though he couldn't see Hope's face from this angle, he could read the rigidness of her posture and the way she stiffened when Brian Elliott patted her shoulder before pulling a chair from a nearby desk and sitting beside her. Pike wouldn't have expected Hope to have friends like that—expensive suits, cocky enough to interrupt the detectives' questions and argue with whatever accusations they were making. He wasn't sure he'd ever seen her with a man who wasn't a customer at her shop. Certainly, the brief scan he'd made of the open rooms of her apartment revealed no signs of a masculine influence in her life. There'd been a flowered centerpiece on the kitchen table and lace curtains masking the blinds at the windows. Not to mention he didn't know any man who liked to see his woman so buttoned up, covered up and pinned up that she faded into the background of his world.

Were those scars he'd glimpsed on her wrist a graphic reminder of whatever her father had done to her? Was that what she was trying to hide? And what was with her dog phobia, anyway? Sure, Hans had been bred and trained to intimidate when ordered to. But otherwise, the big shepherd was a pussycat who couldn't get enough playtime and who regularly conned Pike's mother out of extra dog treats when they went home to visit.

Pike glanced back at the screen. Animal cruelty?

The idea of such an atrocity left a bitter taste in his mouth, especially if that sort of heartless violence had anything to do with Hope's fear.

Pike felt a nudge at his elbow and looked down at the petite crime scene investigator who worked the task force with him. Annie Hermann pointed to the same group he'd been watching. "Why is *he* here?"

He assumed she was talking about her fiancé, Detective Fensom. "Nick? He and Detective Montgomery were the first two detectives on the scene of LaDonna Chambers's rape and murder."

Annie's dark curls bounced around her face as she shook her head. "No, I mean Adam Matuszak. My tall, blond, ambitious ex." She made no effort to mask her sarcasm. Pike liked Annie. She might be a bit of a flake in the personality department, but far and away, she was the smartest, sharpest thinker on their team. She'd been the first to get them a lead on their unsub by identifying his blood type and confirming they were looking for both a rapist and an accomplice who cleaned up after his crimes. "I dodged a bullet when Adam dumped me. She's the bridal shop owner, isn't she?"

"Yeah. Hope Lockhart."

"Does she need an attorney?" Annie asked. "I thought Nick said she was a witness."

"Potential witness," Pike clarified, liking Hope's friends less and less. "Do you know Brian Elliott, too?" The one who kept touching Hope's arm and shoulder, despite the way she subtly shifted posture or pulled away each time.

"He owns most of those buildings in our target neighborhood. He remodels and sells them. If I remember rightly, he invested money to help Miss Lockhart set up her bridal shop. Adam is his personal attorney—

Nick and I met them at a crime scene in one of the buildings Elliott was converting. We thought it might be the location where our unsub was taking his victims to sexually assault them." Annie's voice trailed away and Pike looked down to see where her thoughts had taken her.

"It turned out to be a staged crime scene, right?"

Annie nodded. "It was a trap. If Nick hadn't been there, I could have died."

His attention shifted back to Detective Montgomery's desk, and Pike saw Nick Fensom grab his leather jacket off the back of his chair and excuse himself from the conversation. Hope turned to see where he was going and her gaze locked on to Pike's across the room—for about two seconds before Elliott touched her shoulder and forced her attention back to whatever their attorney was saying to Spencer Montgomery. Hope nodded and answered a question. And then she was pointing to a picture in a book of vehicle makes and models on Montgomery's desk

But in those two seconds, Pike had read a plea in those lake-gray eyes. The fatigue of working through the night melted away and he stood a little straighter, leaned a little closer, felt a little more protective. She was part of the neighborhood he guarded; that made Hope his responsibility. And though she'd made it clear she hadn't wanted his help at her apartment, and she wasn't too comfortable having him touch her, her eyes had sent him a different message just now. *Help.*

Just like with Hans, it had been bred into every fiber of his being to answer that call. But help her with what? How? What did she need him to do? Or was he just imagining her distress? He hadn't read any other nonverbal cues she'd been giving off correctly. Shy—not snooty. Afraid of Hans—not him.

This is too much, please come bail me out—or *what the heck are you still doing there staring at me when whatever interest you have in me isn't as mutual as you'd like it to be?*

There was a reason Pike worked with dogs. Communication with them was so much less complicated. Eat. Sleep. Pet. Play. Work.

While Pike debated the mystery of Hope Lockhart and how he should respond, Nick circled around the counter. He shrugged into his jacket before brushing a curl off Annie's forehead. "Everything okay? Matuszak isn't giving you fits, is he?"

With their opposite personalities, Nick and Annie were the last two people Pike would ever have imagined as a couple. But together, they worked. Annie shook her head and smiled. "I don't even notice him when you're here."

Nick grinned. "Good." He shifted his gaze up to Pike. "Seems like Matuszak ought to be answering some questions instead of keeping her from talking. All we want are details about what she saw last night, and her observations of activities in that neighborhood. But as her business mentor, Elliott claims he knows her better than anybody. He says she's 'sensitive and suggestible' and wants to make sure we're not taking advantage of her or scaring her more than she needs to be. It's like facing off against a pair of big brothers."

Sensitive and suggestible? The woman had stood up to what was probably an abusive father and pulled a knife to defend herself from the things that frightened her. She'd gone to the scene of a homicide to confirm the identity of someone she knew. Pike punched Hank

Lockhart's prison record off the computer screen and turned toward Nick. "Hope may not look like it on the outside, but she's tough. She's a survivor."

"I hope so. I'd still like to get her in a room without her entourage to see what she has to say." Nick's shift was long over, too, but he had nothing but a smile when he reached for Annie's hand. "Come on, slugger. I'll drive you to the lab." With a nod to Pike, the couple walked toward the elevators. "See you at the briefing tomorrow morning. Try to get a couple hours of sleep."

"Yeah," Pike answered. "You, too."

Pike groaned when the elevator door opened and three of the five members of SWAT Team 1 stepped out, including Pike's older brother Alex Taylor. Pike greeted Trip Jones and Holden Kincaid, each of whom towered over his vertically challenged, muscle-bound sibling. As adopted brothers, Alex and Pike couldn't look more different, but they couldn't be closer, either. Growing up in foster care together had forged a bond as strong as blood between them.

And Alex took his role as big brother very seriously. He knew Pike should be home at his apartment getting some shut-eye right now.

After sending his buddies on to roll call, Alex combed his fingers through his curly black hair and stretched up on tiptoe to look over the counter where Pike stood. "Where's your better-lookin' sidekick?"

"Aren't you the funny guy." Logging out of the computer terminal, Pike grabbed his ball cap and joined his brother around the front of the desk. "Hans is in his kennel, getting some R & R."

"Looks like you had a long night, too."

Pike scratched at the stubble that shaded his jaw and nodded. "We had another Rose Red rape."

"Ah, hell." Although the task force was specifically dedicated to solving the string of assaults and related deaths, there wasn't a cop on the force who didn't care about catching the perp. "Did the victim survive?"

Pike shook his head. "Looks like the Cleaner got to her. Shot the vic. CSI Hermann thinks LaDonna Chambers was dead before the body was dumped this time." There had been too many innocent victims. He smacked his cap against his thigh and looked across the room to Hope again. A woman like that shouldn't have to live in fear of walking the streets or going to work. "I don't understand why we can't catch these bastards. He hasn't left a single fingerprint at any crime scene, but we've got the accomplice's on file. We've got the rapist's DNA, but there's no match in the system. According to the CSI I was just talking to, the only blood at this scene belonged to the vic. We can't figure out where he takes them to commit the assault or why this Cleaner goes to so much trouble to destroy any evidence of the crimes. It's a sick relationship."

"I don't know what color they were." Was that Hope raising her voice? "He was going too fast. If I had known who he was, of course I would have…" Her hands squeezed into fists on top of Detective Montgomery's desk. "He wore a hat and a surgical mask. His eyes were in the shadows." Matuszak moved in behind her chair, warning the detective not to press his client.

Alex turned to track the object of Pike's wandering gaze. "What's she got to do with it? Montgomery is lookin' intense."

"I know. They're being pretty hard on her. The woman hasn't had any sleep."

Alex tilted him a curious look. "Is she part of your task force investigation?"

"We think she saw the van our rapist uses to abduct his victims. She may even have seen the guy, but didn't get a clear look at him."

"I thought you were a K-9 cop, not a detective. Have you been asking her questions, too?"

Pike studied the toe of his boot for a moment, recalling that unexpected urge to kiss her. But he remembered the stark fear he'd seen in her apartment just as clearly. The knife and the wild eyes had reflected how well his attempt to develop a rapport with her had gone. He raised his head, wondering again if he'd misread her silent plea for help a few minutes ago. She was hanging in there with Montgomery. "Her shop and apartment are on my beat. I answered a call there last night."

Crossing his arms over his chest, Alex leaned back against the counter beside Pike. "Why don't you go over there and do something about it instead of standing here staring like a moon-eyed teenager?"

"What do you mean, do something? I'm not..." Ah, damn. Had Alex picked up on that weird attraction vibe? Without paying any mind to the flak vest and SWAT uniform his brother wore, Pike quipped back, "I can squash you, you know."

"Hey, I'm older than you—show some respect."

"Don't have to."

"I'll tell Mom."

"Mom likes me better."

Alex shook his head and laughed. "Go over there and say something. Offer her a cup of coffee or a ride home. Give her a break from the Inquisition and she'll be grateful. Is she nice?"

"Are you matchmaking?" Pike accused. "Hope and I aren't even friends. She's not my type."

He preferred getting to know a woman who might actually like him.

"You don't have a type. Besides, I don't buy that 'she means nothing to me' line. You're about to crawl out of your skin with worry, so why don't you go over there and do something about it?"

"Alex—"

"You can handle her."

"What does that mean?"

"I know how suave you are with the ladies," he teased, intimating just the opposite. "At the rate you're going, Matt and Mark will be married before you."

"They're still in school."

"That's why I'm helping you out." Alex gave him enough of a push that Pike had to plant both feet to keep his balance. "What are you waiting for, Casanova?"

"Shut up." Pike returned the shove, pushing Alex beyond arm's reach but returning his teasing grin. "It's a wonder you ever got Audrey to say yes to you."

"And yet she did." Alex flashed his wedding ring and cut Pike a break on the teasing. "Follow your instincts, little brother. There's no other way to figure a woman out. I'll see you in a week at Sunday dinner. Grandma and Grandpa will be back from their fiftieth anniversary trip. I warn you—Grandma said there'd be pictures." Alex doffed him a salute and headed toward the conference room. "Good luck."

"Yeah. See ya Sunday."

After he watched Alex rejoin his SWAT teammates, Pike looked across the desks to Hope again. He could do this without his older brother's help. He started walking before he talked himself out of the idea of taking one more stab at proving to Hope that he was one of the good guys. Besides, she'd been up as long as he had, and if he was this tired, she must be exhausted after the emotional ups and downs she'd been through in the past several hours. He'd be doing her a favor to interrupt the grill-fest of questions.

"Yes, LaDonna worked in my office, and yes, I want answers," Matuszak was explaining as Pike approached. "But I don't intend to let any woman I know be hurt like that again. Hope has told you everything she knows more than once. I won't let you put her through anything else, especially something that's not even admissible in court—like this ludicrous idea of hypnosis."

"But if it could clarify some detail from what I saw, then I'd—" Hope began.

"It won't." Matuszak shut her down and squeezed her shoulder at the same time. "You've done enough. If this…animal…gets wind that you're any kind of witness to what he's done, then he might well come after you next."

Sizing up the tailored cut of the attorney's tan suit and his willingness to scare his client in order to keep her mouth shut, Pike circled around him. Someone here was wearing some serious cologne, too. But he remembered Hope's scent was sweet and subtle. And Spencer Montgomery wasn't the cologne type. Another reason not to like these two.

Detective Montgomery acknowledged him as he joined them. "Pike?"

Hope's face was too pale for his liking. The urge to rescue her and change her perception of him flowed even stronger through his blood now. "I was wondering how much longer you'll need Miss Lockhart, sir. My shift's over and I'd be happy to give her a ride back to her apartment."

Hope's head shot up and those long tendrils danced away from her confused expression. "You would?"

"Anytime."

The wealthy entrepreneur Pike already knew to be Brian Elliott stood up to introduce himself. "And you are?"

"Officer Taylor." They clasped hands in front of Hope's face, and when he glanced down at her with a friendly wink, her pale cheeks dotted with color. Was that embarrassment at his teasing show of support or discomfort that he'd forced his way into a conversation that had already gone on too long for her? Pike forged ahead. "Hope and I have a habit of running into each other."

"Yes. I saw how you ran into her in the elevator." Scowling as if displeased by the half embrace he'd witnessed, Elliott diverted Pike's attention to the other man. "This is my attorney, Adam Matuszak."

"We've met."

They shook hands while Brian Elliott continued. "Thank you, but Hope and I are friends. I've known her for several years now. I was the first to notice her talents as a business woman with impeccable taste. I've nurtured that talent and supported her ever since. Adam and I will take her home."

Although Elliott's tone was polite enough, Pike got the idea that some sort of claim was being made. Were these *GQ* and *Forbes* cover models the kind of men Hope preferred to hang out with? The kind of men who made her feel safe? That didn't bode well for a *Field & Stream* kind of guy like him.

Still, he wasn't looking forward to letting Alex know he'd struck out with Hope Lockhart. Again. He made one last valiant effort, dropping his gaze down to Hope's. "Is that what you want? I'll take you out of here right now. Just say the word."

"I…" She glanced up at both her friend and her attorney before adjusting her glasses on her nose and narrowing her gaze at Pike. "It would be more convenient for Brian to take me. He lives in the same neighborhood."

"I drove Mr. Elliott here," Matuszak added, settling his hand on Hope's shoulder. "It's no problem to drive her, too."

Convenient. Not what he'd asked. But the dismissal was clear. She'd made her choice.

So much for Alex's matchmaking. So much for winning Hope's trust.

"Then I'm headin' home myself." He put his cap on and tipped the bill to her. "Ma'am. See you next time I'm on patrol."

Her gaze dropped to the middle of his chest before she nodded. No *thank-you.* No *goodbye.* No *appreciate your concern.*

A nod.

Pike turned away, strolling toward the elevators and trying to figure out what that woman had against him— and why it bothered him so much that she did.

Chapter Five

A solid night's sleep, a run with Hans, a shower and a shave had refreshed Pike enough to stay focused during the task force meeting early Monday morning.

At least, he was physically alert. Unfortunately, there were so many thoughts running around inside his head that he was distracted, anyway.

The graphic crime scene photos that Annie Hermann passed around indicated that the Rose Red Rapist's level of violence had escalated, and that his habitual routine was growing more erratic. It was disturbing enough that LaDonna Chambers had been abducted and sexually assaulted. But there'd barely been any defensive marks on her. Had the initial blow to the head when she'd been blitz attacked and kidnapped rendered her unconscious through the whole ordeal? If so, then why kill her?

Had something upset the rapist's routine and he'd fired the kill shot out of rage? Had the Cleaner, a female accomplice who destroyed evidence of his crimes, upped her game to the extent that she now intended to murder every victim? Was the assault no longer enough violence to sate these perverts' sick needs?

And then there was the guilt Pike had to deal with. CSI Hermann's timeline indicated that Ms. Chambers's

abduction had happened during his patrol shift with
Hans, just a block away from his location at the time.
She'd been taken from *his* territory. On *his* watch. She'd
been a woman working in the neighborhood he'd sworn
to protect. A law student, LaDonna had been taken
from the parking lot outside the firm where she'd been
doing her internship.

Adam Matuszak's law firm.

First impressions of the arrogant blond attorney lingered in the mix of Pike's thoughts, too.

Pike reached down to where Hans dozed on the floor
beside his chair and stroked the dog's warm flank,
automatically seeking that grounding, don't-stress-
unless-you-have-to feeling that working with the clever
German shepherd gave him. But that first encounter
with Matuszak and Brian Elliott still irritated him. Both
men had shut down Hope's efforts to speak for herself.
And while that might have been a legal thing to protect her from volunteering to say or do anything that
might be upsetting or unnecessary or even potentially
incriminating, it stuck in Pike's craw to think that she'd
tried to make herself heard and no one was listening.

And what would he have done if Hope's high-society
buddies hadn't been there to greet her when the elevator doors opened? Tunneled his fingers deeper into that
glorious hair? Eliminated the distance between them?
Kissed her?

Maybe his instinctive dislike for Adam Matuszak
had a more personal, less noble foundation. Maybe what
galled Pike was that he'd made a concerted effort these
past few months to earn Hope's trust and become a
friend, and—with or without Hans at his side—she'd
repeatedly blown him off. Meanwhile, she aligned herself with those two suit-and-tie movers and shakers of

Kansas City society who'd answered her call in the middle of the night.

Sounded a little like wounded male pride.

That was an unsettling thought, too.

"Either he's getting sloppy or she's learning to enjoy the game, too." Spencer Montgomery's stern voice dragged Pike's attention back to the opposite end of the table where the senior detective ran the task force meeting.

Spencer's partner, Nick Fensom, sat immediately to his left. He tossed the pen he'd been rolling between his fingers onto the table and leaned back in his chair. "So they get more violent and we get no closer to solving this damn case."

"That's not entirely true, Nick." Dr. Kate Kilpatrick, the police psychologist and profiling expert who was a member of the team, was ever the voice of cool, calm reason. She patted the thick case folder sitting in front of her. "We're building an extremely strong case against our unsub, with a variety of evidentiary support. We have his DNA and a surviving witness who can identify him by voice and scent, as well as describe the site where the rapes occur—a building undergoing renovations or construction."

"Doesn't do us any good if we can't catch the perp and put him on trial," Nick argued.

Annie Hermann curled one leg beneath her and sat, trying to calm the fiancé she sat across from. "We know exactly the kind of man we're looking for now."

Dr. Kilpatrick tucked her short silvery-blond hair behind her ears, concurring with Annie's facts. "He's most likely OCD—suffering from obsessive-compulsive disorder. The surgical mask Miss Lockhart mentioned fits our profile. He has specific routines. He needs things to be spotlessly clean and orderly. And even though he functions normally in society, he has issues with successful, goal-oriented women. He's been emotionally traumatized by a woman with power over him—a mother, a lover, a boss."

"Blah, blah, blah." Nick voiced his opinions and emotions more loudly than anyone, but Pike had to admit he was feeling the same frustration.

Maggie Wheeler-Murdock, the red-haired officer who was typing notes onto her laptop, and who had a special affinity for talking to the victims of these brutal crimes, looked up from her computer screen. She directed her question to the police psychologist. "Is it possible the shorter time frame between attacks is because the Cleaner has turned the rapes into murders? She's stealing the spotlight from him?"

Dr. Kilpatrick nodded. "That could be the very relationship he's acting out on by going after these women. She's interfered with his routine. And he no longer sees himself as the most dangerous thing out there on the streets."

Pike finally had something to add. "There's danger enough." He felt all eyes at the table turn to him. "When Hans and I are out there walking our beat, you can see the fear on women's faces. It's in the way they walk and carry themselves. A lot of the businesses in that neighborhood are run or staffed by women. Now some of those businesses are closing because of the fear our unsubs have created. Trust me, I'm less worried about the economic impact than I am about what this guy is doing to the confidence of this city." He braced his elbows on the table and leaned toward the rest of the group. "We need to do something now. Go on the offensive. There are too many dead bodies—too many ruined lives—left in this guy's wake."

"Pike's right." Detective Montgomery surveyed the members of his team, sitting around the table. "We need to set up a sting that will draw this guy out."

"We need bait for a sting," Nick pointed out. "We don't have the manpower to track every potential victim he might go after."

Dr. Kate added another bit of reasoning. "It needs to be a woman our unsub sees as a specific threat to him."

Spencer shook his head. "We've only got two surviving witnesses who can implicate him. One of them is in a mental hospital. And the victim Dr. Kate mentioned— Bailey Austin—we can't count on her. Her assault was too recent. She's too fragile to put into a possible face-off with her attacker unless he's behind the glass in a lineup room."

"It doesn't have to be a previous victim, does it?" Maggie suggested. "Can't we put a female officer undercover in that neighborhood who fits his ideal victim? Make her an irresistible target to draw him out?"

"It can't be you." Dr. Kate smiled and nodded toward the baby bump that was already starting to show following Maggie's summer wedding to a U.S. Marine who'd lived in her apartment building.

Nick Fensom's gaze locked on to the dark-haired CSI sitting across from him. "The Cleaner has seen Annie at crime scenes. We have to assume she's shared that information with our unsub. He won't go after one of us."

Kate Kilpatrick agreed. "None of us can assume the role we need. As the task force liaison to the press, I have my face all over the media. He knows I'm with KCPD, too."

Pike flattened his palms on top of the table. The

team's undercover-cop idea wasn't going to fly. "This guy lives or works in that neighborhood. He knows every woman there. He'd avoid a stranger, unless we're talking about embedding someone there for several months."

Detective Montgomery shook his head. "We can't wait that long. He'll have gone after someone else by then. We need to recruit a volunteer from the community—offer her police protection, of course."

Nick Fensom snapped his fingers. "We've got Pike's girlfriend who gave us the info about the surgical mask and a detailed description of what we believe is his van."

What? Whoa. Pike raised his hands and backed his chair away from the table. "She's not my girlfriend."

Nick swiveled in his chair, his teasing grin looking an awful lot like his brother Alex's yesterday morning. "Then why did you hang out at the precinct for six hours after your shift was over yesterday?"

"Hope was my responsibility. I was the first man on the scene after she called Dispatch. I drove her in to HQ. I wanted to see the incident through to the end." Yeah. That was it. He'd stayed out of concern…because he'd be worried about anybody from that neighborhood on his watch. Right?

Clearly thinking through their options, Detective Montgomery adjusted his dark silk tie. "Brian Elliott offered to put her up in his lake house down in Branson, but she refused. She told me she wanted to stay in the city and help in any way she could."

"There you have it." Nick turned back to his partner. "Our bait."

Pike remembered the prison record he'd read. Henry Lockhart's home address had been in a small town close to Branson. Maybe that part of the state dredged up too many unpleasant memories for Hope. That was probably why she'd refused Elliott's offer.

"I'm sure she was talking about testifying in court," Pike countered. "Not…what you're suggesting."

"She's a successful woman," Montgomery argued. "Runs her own business. She's been a resident in the Rose Red Rapist's target neighborhood for a couple of years now. Hell, the press gave our unsub that nickname because of her shop."

These people weren't listening. Hope Lockhart as an undercover lure? Not that she couldn't attract a man's attention—if she loosened a few buttons on her blouse, let down her hair and actually talked to a guy. But that wasn't going to happen. He'd been trying to interact with the woman for months now, and except for those brief seconds on the elevator, all he'd gotten were some curt hellos and a knife pulled on him. "How are you going to get a man on the scene to protect her without making our unsub suspicious? If you look up *spinster* in the dictionary, Hope Lockhart's picture is right there next to it." He knew those weren't the kindest words, but facts were facts. "You can't suddenly throw a cop into her life and have anybody believe it isn't a sting operation."

Dr. Kate moved her hand to the tabletop next to where Pike's hand rested. "Your emotions are more than a little elevated when you speak of Miss Lockhart. Do you have a relationship with her?"

"With Hope?" His protest was sharp enough for Hans to raise his head.

The psychologist nodded. "If there's already a connection between you, we could capitalize on that."

Oh, yeah. He never should have touched Hope in that

elevator. "I'm not in a relationship with anybody. And trust me, if you're going to recruit her, then you need to send someone else to keep an eye on her."

Spencer Montgomery stood at the opposite end of the room, buttoning his suit jacket, looking as though he was about to wrap up this meeting. "Why? Can't you handle some personal protection work?"

"Of course." The dog rested his muzzle on Pike's knee, giving him a look that seemed to question just where this conversation was taking them. "Hans and I can guard a place or a person better than any team of men. But Hope…she's afraid of me—of us." He reached down to rub Hans's head. "And I don't work without my partner."

Dr. Kate was sizing him up as though he were a patient of hers. "Do you want me to talk to her? You know, helping her through these fears is a very legitimate way to deepen your bond with her."

"I don't have a bond."

"But you *do* know her," Detective Montgomery clarified. "You've had conversations?"

"Sort of."

"You've been seen with her?"

"Yeah, but—"

"Anybody else here know Hope Lockhart better than Pike?"

Maggie gave him a sympathetic look over her laptop. "She planned my wedding to John, but I've got desk duty until the baby comes."

Annie Hermann stuffed her files into her bag. "Sorry. Never met her."

"Saturday night's interview was the first time we've spoken." Nick Fensom tucked his pen into the pocket of his leather jacket.

"It's settled, then." Detective Montgomery closed his notebook and zipped it shut. "Make her like you."

"Excuse me?" Pike stood and Hans fell into place beside him.

"You need to become her boyfriend. I can't think of a more plausible way to work a bodyguard into her life."

"She'll never go for that."

"She'll have to if she wants our protection." Detective Montgomery circled the table, indicating a decision had been made. "Kate, you and I can have a discussion with Miss Lockhart this afternoon. We'll make it clear that we need her help to make that neighborhood—this city—safe again."

"Wait a minute." Pike strode around the table to catch Montgomery at the door. "You want me to… date…Hope Lockhart?"

The red-haired detective's cool gray eyes weren't joking. "I want you to move in with her. Pretend you're having an affair. Or better yet, she runs a bridal shop. Pretend you're her fiancé and you're planning your wedding."

"Detective—"

"We'll provide whatever backup you need—keep eyes on her when you can't. But you and Hans are going to be our front men. We can leak that we've got a description of our suspect—drop some subtle clues that lead back to her. We at least have to ask if she's willing to do it."

"You're going to put a civilian in that kind of danger?"

The detective's assessing look included Hans. "She'll have the best protection KCPD can provide."

"Sir, I've never worked undercover."

"You just have to do your job. Be there if and when

our perp comes after her. You'll still be a cop. You'll just be a cop who's in a relationship." Pike had a sinking feeling there was no argument left to be made. Hope *was* their best shot at luring the Rose Red Rapist into the task force's trap. And nobody else here could make the sting setup work. But what a setup. "Make our unsubs believe that Hope Lockhart is your bride-to-be."

PIKE WATCHED SPENCER Montgomery and Kate Kilpatrick pull out of the parking lot at Fairy Tale Bridal to merge with the beginnings of rush-hour traffic, leaving him standing on the sidewalk out front. He looked down at the alert dog sitting beside him. "I guess we're really going through with this, Hans."

Hans tilted his long black muzzle up into Pike's hand, promising his silent support. Whatever his master had to do, they would do it together. Even if it meant taking on a role neither of them had trained for— pretending Hope Lockhart was their happily-ever-after.

Pike looked up and down the street, wondering if any of the people walking to their cars, heading into shops, peeking out of office windows or warming up with a coffee amongst the autumnal reds and golds of the young trees that decorated the rooftop garden of the cafe on the corner had any suspicion of the trap KCPD was laying for the Rose Red Rapist. Was one of them their man, watching him even now and evaluating his appearance at Fairy Tale Bridal? He was the neighborhood cop, right? Would their unsub buy that he and Hope were an item? Would he believe that all those brief encounters with her these past twelve months had led to a marriage proposal and that the extra security on the premises had to do with love and not catching a criminal? There was only one way to find out.

"Fuss." At the German command to heel, Hans jumped to his feet and fell into step beside Pike as he turned back into the parking lot. "Let's do it."

After holding the door for a group of young women who were all chattering at once about the best color for a bridesmaid dress, Pike led Hans into the vestibule of Hope's shop. He paused a minute to inspect the splintered wood around the lock he'd busted to get up to Hope's apartment late Saturday night. The door swung open with barely a push, making him glad she still had the outside entrance and her apartment door upstairs she could lock for security. But he also made a mental note to pick up some wood from the lumberyard to reinforce the lock until he could get the antique door replaced and a new dead bolt installed.

Inhaling a fortifying breath and reminding himself how important this assignment was to KCPD and all of Kansas City, Pike pushed open the door to Hope's shop.

"…Ms. Carter, er, Mrs. Lonergan now, let me off an hour early to come fix your door." A short, wiry man wearing a green uniform shirt and jeans was talking with Hope across the counter at the center of the shop. Pike recognized him as an employee from the florist's shop across the street. The two businesses often handled events together, but this didn't look like a work-related discussion to him. "She worries about you, you know."

The bell ringing above his head announced Pike's arrival, but it was Hans's loping gate beside him that diverted Hope's attention from the conversation and made her cheeks go pale. She might as well get used to having them both around. She'd agreed to this charade, and that included the German shepherd as part of her bodyguard contingency. He sure hoped Dr. Kilpatrick was right, and that helping Hope deal with her fear of dogs was the best way to earn her trust.

Pike pulled off his KCPD cap and stuffed it into his hip pocket as the dark-haired man clicked his tongue against his teeth to startle Hope's attention back to him. "As I was saying, I've got tools and some wood across the street at Mrs. Lonergan's shop. You know I can be pretty handy. Bet I have it all repaired before you close."

"Thank you, Leon." Was that a smile for the other man? When she hadn't even said *hi* to him? How were they ever going to pull this off?

Leon leaned a little closer over the tall edge of the counter. "If I come back tomorrow for another couple of hours, I'll have it looking as good as new. I promise."

Hope fiddled with the belt of the navy blue dress that covered her from neck to knee and sidled to the far end of the counter as Pike and Hans approached. "You're too good to me, Leon. How much do you think it will cost? You still haven't given me a bill for that window-pane you replaced a couple of weeks ago."

"I won't take your money, Hope."

"Technically, you work for Robin, not me. At least let me pay for the materials."

"No, ma'am." The man slid an annoyed glance toward Pike and Hans, dismissing them as an ill-timed official visit, no doubt, before circling around the end of the counter to block Hope's escape—moving from friendly acquaintance to personal-space invader. "But maybe you'll let me take you to dinner tonight?"

"I thought you had dinner with your mother on Mondays," was Hope's gentle reply.

The guy's fingers tiptoed across the counter toward her hand. "I'll make it up to her. She's subbing in a bridge game tonight, anyway. I'm a free man."

Really? Was this guy hittin' on her? Had Pike completely misread her unattached status? Whatever it was, Pike had to nip the potential relationship in the bud. He walked up behind Hope, crossing behind the cash register and computer as though he had the right to do so. "She's got plans. Right, hon?"

Hope flinched at his touch when he flattened his hand at the small of her back. Or maybe it was the dog standing so close that made her visibly shiver. Either way, she wasn't helping establish any kind of cover. "Hans, sit." While the dog plopped down on his haunches, Pike extended a hand around Hope to introduce himself. "I'm Pike Taylor."

"I know you, Officer. Leon Hundley." The twenty-something man shook Pike's hand, but looked as befuddled by his presence in the shop as Hope did. He thumbed over his shoulder at the big display windows that faced the front sidewalk. "I work at Robin's Nest Floral across the street. I help Miss Lockhart out with odd jobs whenever I can. I'm trying to make some extra cash to restore my car."

And to hit on Hope. Was she even aware that Hundley had been flirting? Or was that innocence the way she shut down any man who showed an interest in her? That didn't bode well for the success of this engagement masquerade.

Pike settled his palm at the nip of Hope's waist and let his fingers fan over the ample swell of her hip, silently warning her not to bolt while he made some neighborly conversation with a local. "What kind of car do you have?"

Good. Leon noticed Pike's subtle claim, and retreated to a more impersonal distance. "A '72 Camaro."

"Sweet. Is the chassis in good shape?"

"Yeah. I painted it blue. Look, Hope and I were having a conversation. Did you need her for something?"

"No. Just dropped in to say hi."

Although he made an effort to reclaim Hope's attention, Leon seemed a little less inclined to hang around the shop and chat than he'd been a moment ago. He pointed toward Hans. "Is he an attack dog?"

"He's a police officer. He doesn't get mean or tough unless I do." Pike released Hope and turned, thumping his chest and inviting Hans to rise on his hind legs and prop his paws on him. Ignoring his stinging conscience at the gasp behind him, Pike rubbed the dog's leanly muscular flanks, sending out a shower of tan and black fur. "Do you want to pet him?"

"Maybe another time." The ploy worked. Even though Hans thought he was playing, it made an impressive show and drove the point home to Leon that the two of them weren't going anywhere. While he pulled out his cell phone, Leon backed toward the exit. "I'd better let Mother know I can drive her to bridge tonight, after all. Then I'll get started on that door. I'll let you know how much the new lock costs."

Did Hope notice that Leon had decided to charge her, after all, since she was no longer available for whatever he'd had in mind? And was she really going to stop talking now that he and Hans were here?

"Thanks, man," Pike offered as the wiry handyman headed out the door. "I'd planned to do it myself. But if you need the cash…"

"Right. I'm on it."

The bell over the door chimed before Pike put Hans in a sit position and turned to apologize to Hope. "Don't worry, I'll clean up where he shed."

But she'd already put half the length of the store

between them and was gathering up a rainbow of fabric samples from the seating area in front of a trio of mirrors.

"Hans, *platz*." Burying his frustration on a gruff sigh, Pike told the dog to lie down and strode across the shop to join her. He picked up a box from the end of one couch and had it ready for her when she turned around with an armful of filmy material.

Hope hesitated for a moment, her gaze darting back to the counter, then up to him before dropping the samples into the box. "So, how do we do this?"

He wasn't sure if she was talking about baiting a trap for a rapist or masquerading as the woman Pike Taylor loved. "I don't know. I think we just have to be seen together. Make it look like we're a couple so no one questions me being here. And don't let the handyman across the street flirt with you."

"I wasn't letting…" She grabbed the box from his hands and carried it into the dressing rooms. "Leon was flirting?"

How could a woman who must be in her early thirties be so sweetly clueless? "He wants something from you."

"Money for his car. A friendly diversion, maybe. His mother has a chronic illness. She makes a lot of demands on his time, and the medical bills don't leave anything extra for fun things—like his car. I try to help out when I can."

"Well, you need to stop providing *fun* for Mr. Hard Luck out there." Pike propped his hands at his belt when she reappeared, carrying three bridesmaid dresses. "The press leak will go out tomorrow morning. In the meantime, Hans and I will keep our eyes and ears open for any sign of our unsub. You do understand what we're asking of you, right? It won't be a cakewalk."

"You met my father. I've been victimized before, Officer Taylor." She hung the dresses up on a nearby wall before facing him again. "I refuse to be a victim again. I'm tired of losing people I know. I'm tired of living in fear."

"That's the first thing that has to change."

Her cheeks warmed with a hint of temper. "I know I don't come across as a very forceful personality, but I do have convictions—"

"I meant calling me Officer Taylor instead of Pike or Edison or Eddie or whatever you decide on."

"Oh." The blush faded. "Like when you called me *hon* in front of Leon." So she had been paying attention and hadn't gone into a frozen version of her last panic attack. With a nervous adjustment to her glasses, Hope went back to the counter, walking a wide berth around Hans even though he had laid his head down to rest and didn't seem to care. "I'm just Hope. The only nickname I ever had was 'Sis,' and you could hardly call me that."

"That's right. You said you had a brother."

She nodded and picked up a computer pad. She brushed her finger across the screen and pulled up a calendar. "Harry. Henry Lockhart Jr.—named after our father. But he doesn't claim that name. He's just Harry. He's a sergeant in the Marine Corps—an MP at a base overseas."

Pike joined her behind the counter, subtly positioning himself between her and the dog. "Then let's just agree that it's Hope and Pike for now."

"All right."

"Besides your dad, is there any other family I should know about?"

"He's not family. Not to either of us." She uttered the statement like a pledge, then set the computer pad back on the counter and tilted her face up to his. "And no, it's just me here in Missouri. Detective Montgomery said that would help make this—us—more convincing. No one should question it."

The bell jingled above the door again. Hope smiled and nodded as a mother and daughter came in. The younger woman hurried toward a princessy wedding dress in the front window and the mom followed. "Excuse me, I have an appointment."

"And we need to make our rounds. Hans. *Steh.*"

Hans jumped to his feet and Hope dived back a step, gripping the counter behind her. "You talk to him in German?"

Pike nixed the idea of telling her that leaping up onto the counter wouldn't stop Hans from getting to her if the dog wanted to. "He's bilingual. He answers to English when he's relaxed like this. But yeah, his work commands are in German. I'll teach you a few words sometime."

"Why?"

"Hans goes wherever I go, Hope. So that means you're stuck with both of us. I want him to mind you as well as me. He'll be our first line of defense if our perp comes after you." He dropped his voice to a whisper the two customers couldn't overhear. "Still want to go through with this?"

She answered with a jerky nod. "If I can help catch that predator, I want to."

Hope's skittish reaction had garnered the mother's and daughter's attention. Pike offered them a reassuring nod before glancing over to see Leon Hundley watching them, too, from the vestibule where he was measuring the broken door. Finally, he turned to the pale woman with the prim dress and too-tight bun. "I'll be back before you close. I'll have an overnight bag with me, and Hans's kennel. We'll talk more then. Lay down a few ground rules."

Pike pulled out his cap and started to leave. But with the customers and Leon watching, he knew he couldn't just walk away. *Might as well go for it.*

In two long strides, he came back. He palmed the nape of Hope's neck, catching his fingers beneath the bun, loosing a few of those decadent curls before tilting her face up to kiss her. Their lips were touching, but she wasn't kissing him back, and he supposed the hand she braced against his chest might look as if she was holding on to him. But she wasn't.

He raised his head, watched her pupils dilate behind her glasses and reminded her they were a team on this undercover op. "You might want to make this look good," he whispered.

When her hand slowly climbed up the placket of his shirt, Pike dipped his head and kissed her again. This time, her fingers curled into his collar, tugging on his shirt and the turtleneck he wore underneath, catching on the edge of his flak vest and pulling him closer as she stretched up on tiptoe. Her soft mouth parted beneath his, but did little more than submit to the force of him pressing against her.

She'd latched onto the front of his shirt with both hands by the time he lifted his head and pulled away. Her breath blew against his lips with a gentle, stuttering whisper of heat. What the heck? He felt that tiny caress like a kick in the gut as he pried her fingers from his wrinkled uniform. This was a charade, wasn't it? So why was he transfixed by those deep gray eyes peering at him over the top of her glasses? Why wasn't he moving away?

It took a nudge from Hans to get Pike to pull his fingertips from the silky bun that wasn't so tight and neat anymore. Pike plopped his hat on his head and tipped the brim before grabbing Hans's leash and heading for the door. "I'll see you in an hour."

That ought to get some tongues wagging about his claim on Hope Lockhart. That soft, shy kiss, so at odds with the fingers grabbing at his chest, had certainly piqued *his* interest.

Chapter Six

"What in the world...?" Hope shielded her eyes and squinted at the bright square of light dancing on her bedroom wall. She picked up her glasses from the nightstand and put them on as she shuffled to the window to peek outside. Normally, the morning sun flooded her apartment with soft warmth and sunshine. It was one of the reasons why she'd converted this half of the second floor into her living space and had left the back half to be used as more storage for the shop below.

But today the clear autumn morning was playing tricks. While the windows facing her across the street remained dark and opaque in the shadows, the sun glinted off the windshield of a vehicle parked below on the street, nearly blinding her. For one frightful moment, her stomach clenched. Was that a white van parked in front of her shop? Was the man sitting behind the wheel watching her shop? Watching her?

A car drove past and she had to close her eyes and turn away. The light bounced from glass to glass and reflected up to her bedroom. No doubt that was the explanation for the dazzling rainbows shining in that had wakened her before the alarm. When her eyes had adjusted and she could lower her hand, Hope saw that the boxy vehicle below was a silver SUV of some type.

Not the van that had followed her home.

Breathing a sigh of relief, she shut the blinds behind the eyelet curtains and considered crawling back into bed. But she had a business downstairs that wasn't going to open itself. And she had an even more important job to do today—help catch a rapist. Detective Montgomery had said she was the city's best chance at ending the nightmare that stalked her neighborhood.

And just like on that fateful morning twenty years ago when she'd made the decision to find help for her starving, neglected brother and herself, Hope knew she couldn't hide in her room and wait for someone to rescue them. She had to venture out and save herself.

Hope tied her blue chenille robe snugly around her waist and took a deep breath before leaving her room. The polished oak planks that ran the length of the entire loft were cool beneath her bare feet. The automatic coffeemaker in the kitchen was bubbling to life and filling her apartment with the rich, warm aroma of fresh java.

But the same odd light was bouncing through her living and dining room area now. When it sliced across the white pillars and exposed brick and hit her eyes again, she tiptoed to the bank of windows facing the street and looked down. As she pulled aside the curtain and leaned closer to the pane of glass, trying to make out a face to go with the gloved hands on the steering wheel below, she heard the engine revving to life. The silver SUV pulled out of its parking space and headed down the street—not an early riser coming to work, but a late-night partier finally going home, most likely.

Funny. Generally, the patrons of the nightspots down the block and around the corner parked in one of the garages down there. It wasn't unheard of on a busy weekend to see cars parked this far up the street, and even in her private lot outside the shop. But on a Tuesday morning? Her heart rate kicked up a notch. Maybe not so funny. It was perfectly likely that the man she'd seen Saturday night had more than one vehicle. He was probably too smart to come back to her place in the van she'd already seen.

"You're making too much of it," she whispered against the glass, trying to calm her racing pulse. "He wasn't watching you. You don't even know it was him."

Still, the nervous instincts refused to completely dissipate. Reflecting lights and unfamiliar vehicles weren't the only differences in her regular morning routine. She had other reasons to be a little jumpy this morning. Her homey, countrified decor now included a large gray kennel with a steel mesh gate. The smells in her home were different, too. There was a slight pungency of dog food and heat from the beast dozing in said kennel. Even the sounds were different. In the early morning quiet before downtown Kansas City came to life again, she heard a soft, even snore coming from her guest room.

Maybe she *should* report the SUV. Just in case she was right to be worried about strange vehicles parked in front of her shop. A panic attack was embarrassing. But not responding to a real threat could be downright dangerous. Her footsteps took her back down the hallway.

She'd made a deal with KCPD—for LaDonna Chambers, for her late friend Janie Harrison, for her client Bailey Austin, for the women who lived and worked and played in this neighborhood, to end that threat. She'd made the deal to help capture the Rose Red Rapist for herself. Because she deserved to feel safe in her own home and shop. She'd gone to bed a shy woman who lurked in the background of society, and she'd woken up to a very different, unfamiliar world where she had to take action and play a starring role.

Hope paused outside the second bedroom and pushed the sleepy tumble of hair off her face. As much as her heart and conscience wanted to do this undercover job to help the police, her father's voice inside her head was telling her she was doomed to fail. She could never pull this off—being the fictitious fiancée to one of Kansas City's finest, playing the part of would-be witness to draw a dangerous man into KCPD's trap.

"You're too much of a coward, girl. Now quit thinkin' on your own and dreamin' those stupid dreams, and do what I tell you."

"Shut up, Hank," she whispered, pushing open the door and peeking inside. She'd gotten her brother away from their father's prison. She'd started her own business. She supported herself more comfortably than she'd ever dreamed possible back on that remote patch of land in the Ozark woods. She could do this, too. She could live with a man for a few days. She could tolerate his dog and get used to their habits. She could even learn to be more convincing as half of a couple.

Still, her heart beat faster and her breath locked up in her chest when she saw the big man sleeping in the bed. Pike Taylor's broad shoulders and naked chest seemed at odds with the white, eyelet-trimmed sheets and hand sewn quilt draped around his waist. A more familiar light coming through the eyelet curtains at the window dappled his skin with tiny spots of sunshine, highlighting golden spikes of hair among the sandy shades of tan and brown on his scruffy jaw and chin, and farther down, in the hair that dusted his chest and narrowed into a thin line running down his flat stomach and disappearing beneath the sheet.

Watching a grown man sleep was as mesmerizing as it was unfamiliar. Other than her brother, Harry, her father ages ago, or catching an accidental glimpse of a customer trying on a tux in her changing rooms downstairs, half-naked men weren't something she'd had much experience with. She'd never had that much muscle and testosterone sleeping in her apartment.

Hope's skin suddenly burned beneath her nightgown and robe, and her mouth went dry. She was assuming Pike Taylor was only *half*-naked. What if he wasn't? Her pulse thundered in her ears. She'd certainly never had *that* in her apartment.

The twin bronze medallions that marked him as uniquely male had puckered in the cool air and stood at attention atop the even rise and fall of his chest, mocking her inability to make a decision. Should she wake him up to tell him about the car? Politely retreat until he was awake and back in uniform?

They probably should have talked about the bathroom schedule and sleeping regalia last night while they were discussing ground rules for this charade. What if he was a sleepwalker? What if he sat up in bed right now and the quilt drifted farther south?

"It's not polite to stare."

Hope gasped as Pike's deep, husky voice startled her from across the room. He was awake? He'd been watching her…watch him? One blue eye blinked open, confirming the worst. Embarrassment heated her face as the second eye opened. "There was a car out front," she blurted. "It's gone." *Sound like an idiot much?* "I'm sorry." She was already backing from the room, pulling the door closed behind her. "I am so sorry."

"Hope? Wait. What car?"

Smooth, woman. She tucked her robe together at the neck and dashed to the kitchen. His teasing tone made it sound as though she'd been admiring the scenery. She hadn't been, had she? Not intentionally. She'd been curious. Concerned. She was just trying to get used to having a man in her home so she wouldn't freak out like... like the way she was doing right now. "Good grief."

If Pike had any doubts about her ability to pretend she was in love with him, she'd just confirmed them.

"Hope?"

She spun around the corner in her haste to get away from the door opening behind her. Her hip bumped a chair and rammed it against the table, knocking the lid off the sugar bowl and waking up the beast sleeping by the front door. Hope shrieked at Hans's deep woof and reversed course, plowing into Pike's bare chest.

Her fingers brushed across ticklish hair and warm sinew before she flattened her palms against a sculpted swell of muscle and pushed away. The heat of his skin sizzled beneath her cool hands and her vision swam with a blur of faded blue. Hope realized he had on a pair of old jeans, and the words tumbled out of her mouth before she could stop them. "Thank God, you're wearing pants."

"Huh?"

The dog barked again, either at her flighty distress or excitement at seeing his master.

Or the gun he held in his hand.

"Oh!" Hope ducked behind Pike, her fingers sliding around the bare skin of his torso as she tried to put him between her and Hans. The moment she noticed that the skin at the small of his back was smoother than the hard muscles of his chest had been was the moment she realized she was still touching him. Hope curled her traitorous fingers into her palms and clutched them beneath her chin. "Sorry. I shouldn't keep grabbing you."

"You shouldn't keep apologizing, either." Pike turned, filling her vision with his broad shoulders and chest. "It's okay. I won't break."

"No. Obviously, you're strong enough to…" Heat radiated off him in waves. Or maybe that was her own embarrassment making her feverish. "I was just caught off guard because you're hot." What did she just say? "I mean, your skin's hot. Temperature-wise. Oh, God."

He reached out and squeezed her shoulder, thankfully silencing her double entendres, keeping the heavy black gun he carried pointed down at his right side. "It's okay. I'm flattered more than I should be. Now tell me about the car you saw."

Those clear blue eyes were all business when she looked above the bare chest. Hope nodded as some of the fluster faded. She knew how to respond to that. "A silver SUV was parked out front when I woke up. I wouldn't have noticed it except the sun was reflecting off the windshield and coming into my bedroom. There was a man behind the wheel, but I couldn't see him well because of the glare." Pike was already moving across the apartment to peek out the front windows. "It's gone now."

"Did he see you look out the window?"

Pike's concise movements made her think she'd been right to be suspicious. "From my bedroom, maybe. If he was looking up. He pulled away when I opened those curtains there."

"He drove south?"

"Yes. Is that a bad thing?"

"I'll find out. Come on, big guy." Hope hugged the

white pillar beside her couch as he released Hans from his kennel, hooked the leash to his collar and opened her front door. "Stay put. Lock the door. We'll be back."

As soon as the door closed, Hope hurried after them to throw the dead bolt. She heard the doors opening downstairs and dashed to the windows to see Pike and Hans rush out to the sidewalk below. Even with Pike barefoot and wearing holey jeans, there was something powerful, vigilant, relentless about the pair's quick movements and watchful scans. They moved up and down the street, following Hans's nose before disappearing around the side of the building into her parking lot.

Several more minutes passed, giving her plenty of time to imagine a dozen different dangerous scenarios, before she heard them on the stairs again. Hope met them at the door and opened it, standing behind its blockade while Pike wrestled for a few seconds with Hans, then tossed a thick rope with a rubber ball tied to it into the living room, where the dog curled up on her braided oval rug to chew on his toy.

"There's no sign of anybody watching the place now." Pike pulled the door from her hands and locked it, exposing her hiding place before she was certain the loose dog wouldn't notice her here. But that long-ingrained phobia was of little consequence. Pike tucked the gun into the back of his jeans and started rummaging through her kitchen cabinets. "You've had company. There were footprints in the landscaping around your lot."

Hope hugged her arms around her waist. "They could be from patrons coming or going to the bar or coffee shop on the corner last night," she suggested.

"They park on the next block and take shortcuts through one of the alleys or my parking lot."

Pike shook his head. "Hans found deep footprints in the mud. Someone was standing there a long time. Facing your shop."

Shivering at the possibility that she hadn't imagined someone outside was watching her, Hope inched into the kitchen with Pike. "Can I help you find something?"

"A trash bag? This was left outside the door." He pointed to a padded envelope he'd set on the table. "I want to bag it for evidence, just in case it's important. Unless you recognize it?"

Hope shook her head. "Under the sink." She looked at the package without touching it. Her name. No return address. No postmark, either.

"Hand-delivered," Pike agreed as if she'd voiced her suspicion out loud, and shook open the plastic bag. "Just like the box of bugs. I'm guessing that whoever was loitering outside was hoping to see your reaction when you open it."

"Should I?"

"Careful. Hans seemed to think whatever's inside would be fun to play with. He didn't indicate anything explosive." Pike waited beside her while she picked up a knife and sliced open the end of the slightly bulging envelope. "Maybe it's another gift from your father?"

"I don't know if I would recognize his handwriting anymore. It was pretty illegible, like this address. But we don't even know if the bugs were from him, do we? He denied sending them."

"Most criminals would." When she glanced up, Pike shrugged an apology. "I did a little research after he threatened you the other night. I know he spent time in Jeff City. Did he ever hurt you?"

Not exactly. Hope tucked her chin to her chest and focused her attention on the envelope again. Hank Lockhart might never have laid a hand on her, but then, he'd never needed to. There were other, far more cruel ways to get an already meek child to do what a man wanted.

"Hope?"

She ignored the curious prompt and opened the package, crinkling up her nose at the rotten odor that suddenly filled the air. "I know that smell." She recognized it from one of the nasty jobs she'd had as a little girl, when her father had been too drunk to clean their tiny kitchen, and what food they'd had in the house had been too precious to share. As much as she wanted to throw the envelope away, Hope knew she had to look inside. But she prayed she was wrong. She wasn't. "Oh, my God."

"Son of a…"

Brown and furry and stiff as a board.

Hope gasped and stuffed the envelope with the dead mouse into the trash bag and scooted across the kitchen. She dropped the knife into the sink and pumped the soap to wash her hands, even though she hadn't actually touched the frozen-eyed critter.

"Hope?" Pike wrapped up the offending present and set it out of sight. "Does that or the bugs mean anything to you?"

"Mean? It means there's some sicko out there having way too much fun at my expense." She washed the knife as well, then dropped it into the dishwasher and rinsed out the entire sink, working frenetically to cleanse the frightening image from her memory.

"I'm talking about those specific gifts. Do they have any significance to you? Any hidden message?"

"I don't know."

"Hope." Pike's hands closed over her shoulders. "You need to calm—"

"No, I don't!" She spun in his hands and shoved him away. The dog jumped to his feet in the living room and barked a warning. Hope screamed and backed against the sink, hugging her arms to her chest and staring straight down at Pike's bare toes. "I'm sorry. I didn't mean it. I'll be quiet."

"Hans. Box!"

Hope flinched at Pike's sharp command, but the dog trotted obediently to his crate and curled up inside. Her gaze made it up to the belly button above the snap of Pike's jeans. "I'm sorry. I shouldn't have pushed."

"Don't apologize for having a temper. I'd be pissed off, too, if someone was sending me those crude gifts and spying on me." After closing Hans in his kennel, Pike reached for her, but grumbled something beneath his breath and pointed to the windows, instead. "Be afraid of that guy out there. Not me."

"I am."

"Which?" He braced his hands at the waist of those softly worn jeans. "You're afraid of him or me?"

Maybe she was just afraid, period. Shaking her head, Hope circled around the table to avoid him, needing time to regroup, rethink, maybe just start this whole day over again. "I'm going to shower and get dressed now. There's cereal, milk and fruit for breakfast. Coffee's made."

But Pike blocked her path when she tried to slide past him, and she had to curl her toes into the cool wood planks beneath them inside her slippers to keep from bumping into him again. "Hope, I don't need you to be quiet or to act like you don't think or feel like anyone else. I need you to talk to me. If we can't learn to communicate with each other, then I'm not going to be able to protect you. And we have to be able to be in the same room together without you bolting, or we're never going to convince anyone we're a couple."

"I know. That's why you need to find someone else to help you."

"There *is* no one else." He scrubbed his palm over his beard stubble, then leaned in, pleading or venting, demanding something she wasn't sure she could give. "This mission has already started. Someone is already watching you—watching us. Now, I know you're a society lady and I'm working-class good ol' boy, but we have to make this happen. We have to make *us* work or our perp will see right through what we're trying to do, and he'll go even deeper into hiding. How many more women will he have to hurt before we get a chance like this again?"

Frowning, she tilted her gaze up to his. "Society lady?"

Those deep blue eyes were dead serious. They could lose the Rose Red Rapist if she couldn't move past her fears and phobias and become a part of the team Pike Taylor needed her to be. Embarrassment faded. Doubt lingered. Yet the determination that had made her say yes to this plan in the first place was still there, beating steadily through her veins. Suddenly she didn't see the half-dressed man who made her so nervous, but the comrade-in-arms whom she was letting down—and the mission they couldn't afford to fail.

"Pike, I'm not a society lady. Maybe I work with a lot of them, but I grew up in the backwoods of the Ozarks. I worked my way through college. I borrowed money from Brian Elliott to buy this building and open my shop, and I'm still paying him back. I'm not… I don't…" Hope shoved her fingers through her hair and gathered it out of the way down her back. "If I concentrate, I can control the panic. I'll learn how to kiss you and have meaningful conversations and pretend I'm not afraid of Hans. Don't give up on me yet. Please. I can do this."

"Give up on you? Why would I…? Oh, Hope." Pike brushed aside a tendril that had escaped from her grasp and tucked it behind her ear. "Have you ever been with a man?"

All the blood seemed to rush straight to the cheek and ear he'd touched. She turned back into the kitchen, confessing the awkward truth. "Pike, I've never even been in a serious relationship." She stared at the turquoise glass tiles of the backsplash before reaching for a bowl of fruit and a clean paring knife. She pulled down two cereal bowls and sliced up a peach into them, needing to keep her hands busy while she talked. "I have friends who are men. And I've dated a few times—mostly business acquaintances, a couple of times in college. But if I ever felt anything more, it wasn't mutual. Or they just wanted… And no, I've never done that, either." When the peach was done, she peeled a banana and kept working. "I don't turn heads. I don't get much chance to practice. All I do is freak out when a dog comes into the room or a man tries to touch me. KCPD may have made a mistake in asking for my help."

He leaned his hip against the counter beside her, glancing around the remodeled loft. "I don't think so. You came from the hills of nowhere and ended up here? You're obviously a smart woman who knows how to work hard and succeed. You're very observant of what goes on around you." He plucked a peach from the nearest bowl and took a bite. "You don't need to say a lot of words for me to know you care about people. You're a champion of this neighborhood. You stood up to your dad the other night, so I know there's strength in you."

She stopped slicing fruit just to listen to his quiet, deep-pitched voice. His words were soothing, supportive, tapping into some of that strength inside her and making her believe, just a little bit, what he was saying. When he reached over to touch her hair again, she tilted her chin up to see his eyes watching the curls sifting through his fingers. "If you left your hair down natural like this, men would notice you. Heck, if you didn't work so hard to hide all those curves, you'd be beatin' us off with a stick."

Hope chuckled at that improbability and he smiled in return.

"You'll never convince me you're anything but a lady. I just need to teach you a thing or two about how we should interact, so I don't startle you or make you too uncomfortable. It won't be hard. Trust me, I'm not that complicated."

She sighed with regret. "But I think I am."

His teasing smile never wavered as he straightened away from the counter. "You've already mastered step one. You called me Pike without even thinking about it. And I think we're having a meaningful conversation right now." He took her hand, setting the knife down on the counter and turning her to face him. Her eyes widened as he placed her hand against that warm, beautiful—bare—skin again and held it there. "Let's work on step two."

He gently pinched her chin between his thumb and index finger and tilted her face up as he dipped his head. "Don't hold your breath," he whispered, seeing she was doing just that. "Relax." Impossible. Not if he was going to kiss her again. He stroked the pad of his thumb over the seam of her lips. "Shh. Easy."

Her lips parted on a breathy exhale and he closed the distance between them, settling his mouth over hers in a gentle kiss.

Hope stilled despite the warmth of mingling breaths and the unfamiliar pressure of his mouth pushing, withdrawing, tugging her bottom lip between his. She concentrated simply on breathing, in and out through her nose. But it was difficult to focus and her breath stuttered. Pike traced his tongue around the rim of her lips, eliciting a sigh, waking nerve endings she didn't know were there. She attuned her senses to the supple firmness of his lips and the soft abrasion of his beard stubble rubbing against her softer skin. He generated such heat wherever he touched her, the curious friction between them stoking something deeper inside, something even warmer than the brand of her fingers splayed over the drumbeat of his heart.

"Like I said—I won't break," he coaxed, kissing the lower curve of her mouth, then the bow on top. "You try," he whispered against her, his warm proximity making her feel connected even when their lips were no longer touching. "I'll go with the flow of whatever you're comfortable with. You're in control."

With a subtle nod, Hope pushed her mouth against Pike's again. She dug her fingers into his chest and circled her left hand up behind his neck, anchoring herself as she pulled up to compensate for his greater height. Her fingertips discovered the crisp line where his short hair met the nape of his neck. She ran her tongue along his bottom lip as he had done with her. His mouth opened with a husky moan from his throat that skittered along her skin and made her nipples tighten with an answering anticipation. Hope shyly touched the tip of her tongue to his and quickly drew back at the unfamiliar contact with its soft, raspy warmth, only to have his tongue chase hers and invite her to take another sample.

Okay, so this guy was a really, really good teacher. This time she cautiously took her time, sliding her tongue against his, tasting the sweet peach he'd eaten and something more, something that made her whimper and want to move closer—something so potent that it made her heart race and her thoughts go fuzzy.

When she recognized the raw desire coursing through her, Hope pulled back, dropping to her heels and releasing her clinging fingers before she embarrassed herself by forgetting the reason for that kiss. "How did I do?"

"Honey, you're a natural." His hands had worked their way into her hair, and were massaging her scalp. "Knew you were smart. Didn't expect you to catch on quite that fast." His chest heaved in and out in a deep rhythm that mimicked her own and fogged up her glasses. She tilted her eyes up to his over the rims and was surprised at how close he seemed, how close he felt deeper inside her. But his eyes were sparkling with humor, not questions. "Feeling any urge to run away?"

Hope shook her head.

"Good." He grinned before taking a deep breath and pulling back. "I think we might have to practice that lesson again."

For a split second, Hope wondered where she'd gone wrong with that kiss. But he was still grinning while he pulled his cell phone from his pocket and punched in a number. "You're flirting, right?"

"Oh, yeah." Pike winked before turning away and reporting the information about the dead mouse on her doorstep to Detective Montgomery.

Hope couldn't seem to erase the silly smile from her own expression as she finished prepping breakfast. The morning might have had a horribly embarrassing and disturbing start, but her day had improved dramatically. Not only was she in the same confined space with a trained German shepherd, but she was entertaining a distractingly shirtless man in her apartment—and not freaking out about either one.

Hope was setting two mugs of coffee on the table when the intercom beside the door buzzed, announcing she had a visitor outside. Glancing at the clock on the stove, she frowned. "Who could that be? The shop doesn't open for another hour. My first scheduled appointment isn't until ten."

Still on the phone with Detective Montgomery, and his hand back on the gun tucked into his jeans, Pike crossed to the window and peeked out. "There's a news van parked outside."

"Already? I thought I'd have some time to prepare…" for the onslaught of attention Dr. Kilpatrick had said she should expect once her name was leaked to the press as a possible connection to the task force investigation. "What am I supposed to say?"

When she approached to see for herself, Pike put out his arm, warning her to stay out of sight behind him.

"Yes, sir. Understood." The intercom buzzed again, making her think of a timer that had just run out. There was no backing out of this now. Hope looked up to Pike for guidance. He tucked his phone into his pocket and nodded to the intercom. "Go ahead and answer it. Get a name and find out what they want."

Aware that Pike was following right behind her, Hope cleared her throat, then pushed the call button. "Yes?"

"Miss Lockhart? Hope Lockhart?" A smoothly modulated woman's voice answered.

"Who's this?"

"Vanessa Owen. Channel Ten News. I've been to your shop before, remember? Right after Bailey Austin was assaulted?"

"I remember you, Ms. Owen." The dark-haired beauty had practically become a fixture in the neighborhood this past year. The female reporter's tenacious coverage of the Rose Red Rapist attacks and subsequent investigation had made her a staple on the evening news in Kansas City, and had even garnered her some national appearances for her coverage of the crimes. "It's awfully early. The shop isn't open yet."

"I'll wait, Hope. May I call you Hope?" Did she have a choice? "I'm shopping for information, not a dress. You've been holding out on me. I want you to tell me everything you know about the Rose Red Rapist."

"Everything I—?"

Pike pulled her hand off the button to mute their conversation from the reporter. "There's no time for a learning curve here. It's showtime. Are you ready?" Hope was about to be thrust from nobody in the background to headliner of the front-page news. Pike turned his hand into hers and laced their fingers together. "We're a team, remember? You can do this. I've got your back."

After a moment's hesitation, Hope squeezed her grip around Pike's, holding on as she pressed the button again. "I need half an hour, Ms. Owen. Then I'll be down."

Chapter Seven

"This isn't a good time, Hank." Hope had thought answering her phone would give the idea to the stunning brunette reporter that she had a business to run and the interview needed to be over. She'd been wrong.

"Is that the boyfriend?" Vanessa Owen drummed her dark red nails on top of the central counter in Hope's shop.

Boyfriend? Hope snapped her mouth shut as soon as she realized the surprise that must have registered on her face. With a quick no, she turned away from the curious reporter. "I have people here. I need to go."

If she had known it was her father on the line, she would have let it go to voice mail, closed her shop and locked herself in the storeroom until all these people who wanted something from her left her alone. "We're just a few minutes from your place." Hank was in charming mode this morning. But that would change soon enough if he didn't get his way. "Won't be any trouble to stop by for lunch. I'd like to catch up on all the time we missed."

"I'm busy."

"What about dinner?"

"I can't."

"What if I said I was dying?"

"Are you?" She hugged an arm around her waist and dropped her voice to a whisper.

That he didn't answer told her the pang of remorse she'd felt for a split second had been a wasted emotion. The charm bleeding from his voice confirmed it. "What if I said it was about Harry? Would that get you to listen to me?"

"I don't have time for this."

"Girl, I'm your father. I raised you." She'd raised herself. *He* had nearly killed her. "There are certain expectations and responsibilities. You have to talk to me."

"You know, actually? I don't." Hope hung up and set the phone on the counter.

"Oh, good." Seeing that the call had ended, Vanessa Owen wasted no time in asking one more question. "Could you hold that dress up beside you again?" She snapped her fingers to call her cameraman back from the shop's front door. "Damien, make sure you get a picture of this. My viewers will love the wedding dress angle. You see those shows all over cable these days, don't you? Very popular."

"I suppose." Hope blinked against the camera's bright light as she hung up the white gown on the tall hook beside the central counter. She wasn't sure what wedding dresses had to do with an interview about the Rose Red Rapist, but after two hours of questions on everything from why she'd been up so late the night she saw the van to why she thought she hadn't been singled out as a victim yet, Hope was certain Vanessa would use whatever footage and sound bites guaranteed her the biggest viewership.

"Vanessa, how much longer are you and your vultures going to prey on Hope this morning?"

Brian Elliott didn't seem particularly thrilled to have his eleven o'clock appointment delayed by the intrusion of television cameras and reporters still lingering on the sidewalk in front of Fairy Tale Bridal. And even though the bulk of the impromptu press conference had dispersed, he was still irritated enough to follow Vanessa to the counter to vent his displeasure.

"That's good, Damien. I'll be out in a minute." Once the reporter dismissed her crew and turned her big doe eyes up to meet the man who obviously knew her on a first-name basis, Hope seized the opportunity to finally evade the spotlight.

More than once, she'd repeated the information Kate Kilpatrick and Detective Montgomery had encouraged her to share with the media. But no matter what she'd said, her answers never seemed to be quite thorough enough to satisfy the reporters and curious passersby who'd stopped by to see what all the fuss was about. With a wink from Brian, urging her to go on about her business and take the respite she needed, Hope zipped the long white gown into a garment bag.

"Eloquently put as usual, Brian." Vanessa's dark red lips pouted into a smile. "You know I'm only doing my job."

Hope picked up the alterations estimate for her seamstress and pinned it to the plastic bag before draping the dress over her arm. But when she tried to slip away to the dressing rooms, Brian's attorney, Adam Matuszak, was blocking her path.

"Excuse me, Adam."

Two or three seconds passed before she was even sure he'd heard her. Barely taking his eyes off the charged debate between his client and the brunette, the blond attorney stepped aside for Hope to pass—or perhaps just to join the conversation. "You keep show-ing Brian's buildings as crime scenes on the evening news, and you'll put him out of business."

"Adam, dear. Always good to see you." Clearly, all three ran in the same social circle and knew each other personally. Curious as she might be about that tense triangle, Hope skirted around the attorney and carried the dress to the seating area in front of the three-way mirror. She saw Vanessa's smile reflected in one of the mirrors, and wondered if the woman's exotic beauty re-ally was that striking, or if her hair, lips and nails only looked extra rich next to her own mousier reflection. "Why would I want to do a thing like that?" Vanessa asked. "You know how much I enjoy Brian's company."

"I know how much you enjoy Brian's money."

"I'm a success in my own right, Adam. I don't need any man's money."

"You certainly seem to be making a killing on Bri-an's misfortune," Adam argued. "He's trying to re-claim the run-down parts of this city, and all your news stories talk about is the crime spree happening here. Why don't you give some press to the historic pres-ervation and revived economy he's brought to down-town K.C.?"

Hope carried the gown inside the dressing rooms, but the agitated voices were loud enough to carry throughout the shop. She was glad there were no cus-tomers on-site. There was no Pike Taylor on-site, ei-ther, but he had assured her that his detective friend, Nick Fensom, was hiding close by, keeping an eye on her and the shop while Pike and Hans made their rou-tine morning patrol. He'd made a point of walking her down the stairs to greet the reporter and welcome her and her cameraman into the shop, giving Hope a goodbye kiss that had gone beyond their kissing lesson in the kitchen, leaving her gasping with surprise and making sure that anyone who was up and about in the neighborhood could see that shy Hope Lockhart was a spinster no more.

With a silent warning to step up her game and a squeeze of her hand that she thought was meant to reassure her, Pike had left her to face Vanessa Owen and the gathering contingency of reporters and onlookers outside her shop alone. She knew he couldn't stay on the premises around the clock or else the Rose Red Rapist might peg him for the bodyguard he was. Still, it was a little discomfiting to realize just how quickly she'd developed a craving for that boyish grin and the squeeze of his hand around hers. And while she had no illusions that their fake relationship was anything more than a job to Pike, she was beginning to think— and hope, maybe just a little bit—that they were becoming friends.

But they would never be more than friends. Pike was a virile, outgoing, confident man, and she was… well…Hope Lockhart.

She looked in the dressing room mirror and studied her lips. They looked pink and pale compared to the lush burgundy of Vanessa Owen's mouth. The boxy cut of her brown suit hid all the plump curves that more than compensated for the skin and bones child she'd once been. Unbuttoning the top of her cream-colored blouse, Hope pulled aside the collar to look at the faded scars on her neck, shoulder and chest. They were such vivid reminders of not only her traumatic past, but of the cautious, closed-off woman she had become. While she had no trouble being attracted to Pike's tall, muscular body and rugged looks, he certainly had his work cut out for him, convincing the world that he'd fallen so in love with her this past year that he'd moved in.

"You're never gonna amount to anything, girl. Now put those highfalutin ideas right out of your mind and fetch me a beer. That's all you're good for."

"Shut up, Hank." Temper brewed in her veins. When was that ugly voice ever going to stop talking in her head? "I have a job to do. LaDonna and Bailey and all those other victims need me to pull it together." She straightened her collar and refastened her blouse, going back to unhook the top two buttons and let it fall open in a modest effort to play a more believable mate for a man like Pike. She pulled a belt from a returned tuxedo order and cinched it around her waist, nodding approval at the hourglass shape it gave to her figure. "Pike's doing his part." She talked louder than the demeaning voice inside her head. "Stop thinking about who you were and who you wish you could be, and do your part, too."

That meant she couldn't spend the rest of the day hiding in the dressing room, having philosophical discussions with her reflection and avoiding the tension in the other room. Hope picked up three dresses a customer had tried on earlier, and quietly returned them to the racks while the debate continued at her front counter.

Adam had moved closer to Brian and Vanessa, still arguing that the Rose Red Rapist attacks were motivated by some kind of vendetta against his employer. "It's awfully convenient that these assaults have all taken place in this neighborhood."

"Interesting theory," Vanessa drawled, sounding more amused than curious. "You think that these attacks are all part of a giant conspiracy to devalue Brian's investments? Instead of, say, that he lives in this area, or that this is where he can find the successful professional women he targets?"

"I'm just saying there's more than one person benefiting from this guy's reign of terror over the city." Adam pointed an accusatory finger at the reporter. "It put you on the radar of every national news bureau, didn't it?"

"That's enough, Adam." Brian pushed his attorney away in a protective gesture. "Vanessa is only doing her job."

"And I'm doing mine. You hired me to protect you and your interests, Brian. This woman is taking advantage."

"Boys, boys."

Hope watched as the woman in the taupe silk pantsuit stepped between the two men, tapping a dark red nail against both chests.

"You and I will have to discuss the rapist's possible motives beyond terrorizing women sometime, Adam." Vanessa dismissed him before turning to Brian. "Are we still on for dinner tonight?" To Hope's surprise, she stretched up and kissed his cheek, leaving a brand of burgundy lipstick on his skin. "Later. After the broadcast. I'll bring the wine."

Brian took a handkerchief from his suit jacket and wiped away the stain with a handsome smile. "Don't keep me waiting too long."

Hope hugged the last dress she held as Vanessa walked her fingers up Brian's lapel and tapped his lips. More than discovering that her friend and the reporter were apparently an item, Hope was stunned by the woman's smoothly flirtatious moves. Was that the kind of teasing maneuver Pike expected her to make?

That the world expected to see between a couple like the one they were pretending to be? "Don't I always make it worth the wait?"

With a deep sigh, Brian pressed a kiss to Vanessa's finger. "Always. Tonight, then." Folding up his handkerchief and tucking it into his pocket, Brian turned to the tall, dark-haired woman waiting patiently by the front door. "Adam? Regina? Shall we get on with our business?"

Regina Hollister, Brian's executive assistant, stepped forward when summoned. Her eyebrow arched as she passed Vanessa, giving Hope some idea of what the businesswoman thought of her boss's paramour. But any hint of a personal emotion was quickly replaced by cool efficiency. Pulling up the sleeve of her charcoal-gray suit, Regina checked her watch. "I'm sorry, Brian, but we need to go now to make your lunch with the mayor. I'll reschedule your appointment with Miss Lockhart."

Hope hung up the dress and returned to the counter to finish up the meeting that had never had the chance to get started. "That's okay, Brian," she assured him. "I'm a little talked out for the day, anyway."

"I can imagine." Brian buttoned his tailored jacket and leaned in to kiss her cheek, giving her a whiff of the strong cologne he wore. "Sorry we got so sidetracked. We'll work out those easement regulations so you can get that bigger parking lot you want. I know you'd like to get construction started before the winter weather hits."

She nodded. "If I can."

"How about I have Adam pull the necessary permits and construction contracts and have him contact you with some initial estimates? Adam?"

But the attorney didn't immediately respond. He was

at Hope's front window, watching Vanessa strut down the sidewalk, leaving her news van behind. What was she up to now? Where was she going?

Before Hope could come up with any answers, Adam spoke. "What did you say that van you saw looked like, Hope?"

"White. Boxy. Silver bumper."

Adam pointed through the display of fall-colored bridesmaid dresses to the vehicle out front. "You cover up the logos on that van and what do you have?"

Hope walked up beside him. Channel Ten's shiny rear bumper gleamed in the sunlight. The make and model were the same. But that couldn't be the same vehicle, could it? The van she'd identified had rusting wheel wells. She'd seen it late at night, through tired eyes. Could she have mistaken the brown trim for rust in the dark? She adjusted her glasses at her temple and looked through the van's side entry, up to where the cameraman, Damien, sat behind the wheel. He was sipping coffee, steadily meeting her curious gaze through the front window.

Hope recoiled back a step. Damien wore no stocking cap, no surgical mask. But his dark eyes...they watched...

There was always somebody watching.

The temperature in the shop suddenly seemed to plummet. It was probably just the cop outside, protecting her, that she sensed. But this—she peeked through the mannequins in the window, scanning up and down the street—this felt like something more. Something sinister.

She yelped when Brian palmed the center of her back, halting her unconscious retreat. "Enough, Adam.

You're frightening her. Besides, I'm quite certain Vanessa is not the Rose Red Rapist."

"This isn't a joke. I know KCPD is looking for a man." Adam had been studying her reaction, too. "What about someone else on the Channel Ten News team? It wouldn't surprise me if Vanessa knew the rapist's identity and was covering for him so she can keep reporting the story and making headlines."

"That's horrible," Hope whispered. "What woman would do something like that? That monster needs to be put away."

"Mr. Matuszak." The sharp voice of rebuke came from Regina Hollister this time. "On behalf of women everywhere—shut up." Then she looked to her boss and tapped her watch. "The mayor?"

Brian circled around Hope to stand toe-to-toe with his attorney, warning him. "I won't hear another word against Vanessa's character."

Despite his superior height, Adam seemed to understand who paid his salary and relaxed his defensive posture. "You're right, of course. I know Vanessa means something to you. She and I dated a couple of times before I got wise to her. I'm just trying to spare you the pain I went through. As I said before, I'm looking out for your best interests."

A moment more passed before Brian smacked Adam's shoulder and nodded. "That's why I pay you the big bucks, Adam. Thanks. Don't worry. I understand the kind of woman Vanessa is. I've got both eyes wide-open."

What kind of people formed a relationship with someone they couldn't trust? Brian Elliott was an attractive, wealthy man—he could have any woman he wanted. Adam Matuszak, as abrasive as he was, would be considered a catch, too. How did he feel about his boss dating his ex? Was he jealous? Or was he truly concerned that Brian would get burned, too?

And why did they have to bring all their drama into her world when everything was already such a frightening mess?

The bell chiming above the shop's side entrance offered her the diversion she needed to interrupt her thoughts for a few minutes. "Excuse me, I have a customer."

Brian nodded as she left them at the window. "I'll have Regina call you. We'll show ourselves out."

Hope smoothed her hand against her neck, battling the urge to button her open collar and hide like the turtle she was used to being. *Stay out of your head, Lockhart.* She quickly pulled her hand down and headed toward the woman who was admiring a display of beaded evening purses.

She recognized the brassy blonde chauffeur who'd been with her father the other night. So much for keeping her father out of her life. "Nelda, is it?"

"You're Hope, right? We didn't get to meet the other night." Her smoky voice was friendly enough. She extended her hand. "Nelda Sapphire. It's my stage name. For my blue eyes. I'm a dancer. Well, I used to be. I own the place now." She tilted her head to one shoulder, indicating the door. "That's where I met Hank."

Hope wasn't about to judge Nelda on her name or profession or the overprocessed pouf of her hair—only on her taste in men. Had Hank duped Nelda, promising some sort of caring relationship with the same empty words he'd used with his late wife and children? Or was the woman fingering the expensive purses in a business partnership with Hank, working with him to beg or con whatever money they could out of Hope?

A glance beyond Nelda confirmed the worst. The older woman hadn't come alone. Her father stood out in the parking lot, finishing off a cigarette. "How can I help you?"

"You're going to give me a good deal, aren't you?" Nelda's smile seemed sincere. "You know, the family discount?"

Giving Nelda the benefit of the doubt, Hope politely corrected the status of her relationship with her father. "I'm sorry. I think Hank may have misled you if he intimated that I'd be doing him any favors."

Nelda shifted on the ridiculously high heels she wore. "You know your father regrets what happened between you, don't ya, sweetie? He didn't really come to Kansas City for a handout. He wants to work, to earn the money you give him. He's awfully handy with repairing things and cleaning up. It's hard for an ex-con to get a respectable job that pays much. But we thought that maybe, since you're family—"

"No. I'm sorry."

The friendly smile vanished. "Then I hope that lady out there is paying him for all those questions she's asking. We need money."

"What lady? Oh, no."

Hope dashed to the vestibule and pushed her way out the second door to the parking lot before the inner door had fully closed. Why hadn't Vanessa Owen gone back to the TV station? Instead of prepping for the evening broadcast, she stood in the parking lot, shivering against the autumn chill while she chatted with her father—and hung on to every word.

Her father, of course, was eating up the attention. "I

ain't proud of what I done. But I served my time. Hope's stubborn like her mama was. She ain't forgiven me yet. But she's got a good heart. She will."

Forgive? Yes. Her peace of mind demanded it. Forget? Never.

Hope walked up behind her father. "Why are you talking to Ms. Owen? She doesn't even have her coat. I'm sure she needs to get back to the TV station to finish her report."

"Nonsense. I have plenty of time." Vanessa hugged her arms in front of her against the cool temperature, but her smile never wavered. "Your father and I are getting acquainted."

Hank dropped his cigarette to the asphalt and ground it out beneath his boot before facing her. His leathery face creased with a smile she didn't believe. When he reached out to hug her, she put up her hands and backed away. That was a charade she couldn't play. Hank laughed when he turned back to the brunette reporter. "My girl was always makin' up stuff in her head. Like she wanted to be a princess or there were witches in the woods."

Vanessa's assessing gaze darted over to Hope and back. "Do you think she made up seeing the Rose Red Rapist?"

"Well, it's gettin' her lots of attention now, isn't it?"

"Do you think I want this kind of scrutiny in my life?" Hope wondered if Hank could see that Vanessa's amused smile never reached her eyes. She wondered if she smelled booze on his flannel shirt and denim jacket because he'd already been drinking that morning or because he hadn't changed from the night before. "This man is not a reliable source for any news story. I saw what I saw. The van, the driver, everything. I didn't make up any of it."

But Vanessa truly was the shark Adam Matuszak had accused her of being. And she was on the trail of a juicy sidebar to Hope's story. "You've got a bit of a charming country boy accent there, Mr. Lockhart. What part of the state are you from?"

"I asked you to call me Hank, ma'am." He pulled a pack of cigarettes from his pocket and tapped out another smoke. "You ever been down to the lakes around Branson? Deep in the Ozark Mountains?"

"How about I buy you a cup of coffee, Hank, and we talk someplace warmer? You can tell me all about those mountains." She waved to Damien in the news van and pointed down the street before linking arms with Hank and pulling him into step beside her. "Did your daughter grow up there, too?"

"Hank, no one needs to know—" Hope chased after them, but a bright flash of light blinded her as soon as she reached the sidewalk. Hope threw up her hands to protect her eyes, remembering for a split second the mysterious flashes that had wakened her in her bedroom that morning.

"Gabriel."

"Vanessa."

Before Hope could blink her vision clear and push aside her nerves, Vanessa Owen was trading cheek-to-cheek air kisses with a handsome, black-haired man wearing jeans and a corduroy sports coat. The camera and plastic ID badge hanging around his neck identified him as another reporter. "You're a few steps behind on this scoop, aren't you, Gabe?"

"I don't think so."

"Let's do lunch sometime and compare notes."

"Sure." The male reporter watched Vanessa and Hank walk off together toward the coffee shop on the corner before shrugging. "When hell freezes over."

Hope was torn between following her father, to shut him up about the pitiable past she'd overcome, and retreating to the shop to hide from his lies. But the second reporter raised his camera again and she put up her hands to shield her face. "Don't. Please."

"Fair enough." He lowered his camera and pulled out a pad and pen. "Gabriel Knight, *Kansas City Journal*. I got the shot I needed. Unlike my colleague Ms. Owen, I'm not into sensationalism. I'm all about getting the real story." His blue eyes seemed to size her up and find her wanting. "So KCPD finally has a witness who's going to wrap up this fiasco of an investigation for them."

"Fiasco?" The urge to defend the people she was helping proved stronger than the desire to flee. "The task force has made huge strides in identifying the rapist." She repeated one of the talking points Kate Kilpatrick and Detective Montgomery had given her to share. "I'm just one little cog in the wheel that represents all the hard work they've done to protect this city."

"That task force has been pursuing their serial rapist for over a year now. Where are their results? Why isn't a picture of the man you saw splashed all over my front page?"

"I didn't get that good a look at him. The sketch artist's picture wasn't…conclusive. It could start a panic. People might start turning in any man on the street who vaguely fits the description." Hope curled her toes inside her pumps, standing her ground when Gabe Knight tapped his pen on the edge of his notepad before he wrote down whatever observation he'd just made about her.

"But *you* could identify him if you saw him again." His piercing gaze reminded her of the intensity of another pair of eyes, leaving Hope feeling vulnerable, defenseless.

Lying didn't come easily under that challenge. "I think so."

"And the van?"

"Absolutely."

But the reporter was shaking his head. "There's something more going on here. What aren't you telling me?"

She'd spent the whole morning battling Vanessa's questions, and after a few minutes, this man had already done more to rattle her composure. "What do you mean?"

The reporter narrowed his gaze as though studying her through a microscope. "What makes you so special? What secrets are you hiding?"

"I'm not hiding anything." A movement in the corner of her eye turned her attention to the floral shop across the street. Leon Hundley was there in his green uniform shirt, carrying a tray of flower arrangements out to the delivery van. He'd stopped his work, no doubt watching the parade of people in and out of her shop. When their eyes met, he set the tray in the back of his van and took a couple of steps toward her. But his attention turned up the street and he stopped. A moment later, Pike's black-and-white K-9 unit truck was pulling into the parking lot beside her.

But Gabe Knight seemed oblivious of Leon's concerned interest or the brawny uniformed cop climbing out of the truck he'd hastily parked. "A woman who calls her father 'Hank' and hates seeing him walk away with a reporter as much as she hates seeing him at all? There's a story there."

"You were spying on me?" Goose bumps scattered over Hope's skin as she swept her gaze up and down the street. She felt eyes on her even now, and she hated it. The lights, the reporters, her father, her friends…and someone else. *He* was watching her. But from where? Who was he? Someone on the street? Someone hidden? Someone she knew?

"The press conference is done, Knight." Pike loomed up behind the reporter, the broad shoulders of his black uniform dwarfing the other man. "No more questions."

"Pike." Relief crashed through Hope, and she reached for his hand as he came around to stand beside her. She didn't realize how badly she'd been shaking until she felt the anchor of Pike Taylor's grip closing around hers. "I'm glad you're here."

His sharp blue gaze ran over her face. "You okay, honey? Did this guy upset you?"

Honey. Right. He wasn't here to pull her back from the brink of another panic attack. He was here to play the part of the concerned fiancé.

Disappointment joined the roller coaster of emotions that left her feeling drained. But when she extricated her hand from the false comfort of Pike's grasp, he draped his arm around her shoulders and hugged her to his side, as if sensing her retreating into her shell or getting ready to run. "You're cold." When she didn't respond, Pike turned his interrogation on the reporter. "Are you pestering my fiancée, Knight? She agreed to give a statement to the press, but she doesn't have to answer any questions she doesn't want to."

The wall of heat pressed against Hope felt as foreign

as the hard shell of the flak vest Pike wore beneath his shirt. And the crisp, starchy scent of his uniform was more basically male and more enticing than the eye-watering potency of Brian Elliott's cologne had been. Yet the same intriguing sensations that left her feeling so unsettled and out of her depth seemed to fill her with strength and a quieting sense of calm, as well. They didn't have to be a real couple. She could accept comfort from a friend, couldn't she? She could latch onto this much-needed support from her partner on this mission. Slowly, she wrapped her arm behind his waist and leaned against Pike's treelike strength. She was as aware of the gun and handcuffs and other survival equipment strapped to his belt as she was the tapered waist and abundant heat emanating from the man himself. Next to this man, she was safe.

Despite the protective shield of Pike's arm around her, Gabe Knight still didn't seem to be in any hurry to leave. "I have one last question, Officer Taylor."

"What's that?"

The reporter looked up to Pike and down to Hope, then farther down to the hand she clutched at her side. "If you two are engaged, where's her ring?"

Pike's grip tightened on her shoulder, the only indication that he'd been caught off guard by Knight's question. But with eyes watching and her eagerness to get rid of the reporter combining with her determination to get past this crippling timidity, Hope blurted out, "It's at the jewelry store, getting resized."

Pike squeezed her shoulder again, perhaps out of gratitude this time, as he followed her lead. "That's right. It's my grandmother's ring."

Hope flared her fingers in front of her face. "She had small hands."

"I see." Gabriel Knight tucked his pen and pad back inside his jacket. His expression as to whether he believed the ruse or not was hard to read. "Congratulations to you both. I look forward to seeing the announcement in our paper. May I?" Before either of them could answer, he'd raised his camera again and snapped a picture of Hope and Pike standing side by side. "I'll send you a copy." With a nod in lieu of a goodbye, he turned and climbed into a silver SUV sedan parked beside the curb. "So many secrets."

Holding her breath, holding on to Pike, until the last intrusion on her morning drove away, Hope finally inhaled a deep breath that pushed against him. "What does he mean by that? Do you think he knows what we're doing?"

Letting her pull away, though taking her hand so she couldn't immediately leave, Pike turned to face her. "Knight's a sharp one. If he senses there's more to a story, he'll be relentless in uncovering it. Plus, he's been supercritical of KCPD's handling of the Rose Red Rapist case."

"Why?"

Pike pulled off his ball cap and smoothed his hand over his hair. "I don't know. Something makes it personal for him."

Hope trembled at the idea of one more person keeping a closer watch on her than she'd like. "Do you think he'll blow our cover and tip off your unsub?"

The breeze caught a loose tendril of hair and blew it onto Hope's forehead. But Pike's hand was there to smooth it back into place. "We won't let him, okay? What's this?" He traced the same finger along her throat to the notch of her collarbone, tickling her skin as he took note of the extra couple of inches of skin she was showing. "You're changing your looks on me."

He'd noticed the difference of a button and a belt? She hoped that was a good thing. "I was studying other women today, trying to emulate how they dressed and acted around men. I'm trying to be more convincing as your bride to be."

"You did great with Gabe Knight just now. I'm kicking myself that we didn't think of a ring to go with our cover story."

Just then the door to her shop swung open and Nelda Sapphire came running out. Well, *running* was a relative term, considering the way she shuffled down the street in those high platform heels. "Hank! You get back here!" Nelda ran right past them with nary a look or word of acknowledgment. Instead, she clutched her bag beneath her breasts and shuffled it into double time. "Where is he going with that woman? You're not leaving me! You owe me!"

The cursing blonde climbed into her compact car and made a U-turn to follow Hope's father down the street. Pike thumbed toward the car as she drove past. "Promise me you'll never change to that extreme."

Hope drew in an easier breath and smiled with him. "I won't. I couldn't handle the shoes."

Pike's laughter faded as he tucked his cap into his back pocket and settled his hands at the nip of her waist. He pulled her half a step closer, dipping his face toward hers to whisper, "Seriously, though. Are you okay? I had no idea the reporters would still be here. Nick gave me a call and said you had some hangers-on. When he described your dad and Blondie there showing up, Hans and I booked it back over here."

"Hans is in the truck, I'm assuming?" Hope debated

where to rest her hands in order to complete this public embrace for whatever audience they had. Her hands bobbed from Pike's shoulders to his biceps and finally came to rest against the Kevlar armor on his chest.

He nodded. "You didn't answer me. How are you doing?"

She stared straight ahead at the contrast of her pale hands against his black shirt. "Pretty well, I think. I haven't run away or pulled a knife on anyone—yet." Instead of laughing at the joke, Pike fiddled with that stray curl again, silently waiting for her to continue. "I said everything Dr. Kilpatrick and Detective Montgomery asked me to. I'll be on television and in the newspapers. The whole city is going to know who I am now. *He's* going to know."

Hope was decidedly uncomfortable standing in the circle of Pike's arms in front of her shop where anyone on the block could see them. And while his abundant heat and gentle hands excited something feminine and fascinating and unfamiliar in her blood, it was the movements and shadows in windows and vehicles along the street that really made her nervous.

"Do you feel it?" She voiced the tension humming through her.

"Feel what?"

"Someone watching." She tipped her head back to see his sharp gaze swinging back and forth. He was looking, too. "Do you think I'm paranoid?"

That clear blue gaze settled on her. "No. I've felt it, too. Since moving in last night. Like we're living in a glass house. Someone's got to be watching the place to know when they can drop off those creepy gifts without me seeing him or Hans hearing him. But just the same..." His hands tightened at her waist and he pulled her into his chest, winding his arms behind her back and resting his chin at the crown of her head.

Her arms caught between them and she whispered against the KCPD logo embroidered on his chest, "Did you see someone? What do you need me to do?"

"Easy, partner. I need you to let me hold you for a minute. I need to know that you're safe and that this isn't the craziest idea KCPD ever had." Pike's fingers slipped into the hair at the nape of her neck and tugged several curls from the clip she wore. Then they tunneled beneath to cup her head and pull her more snugly against him. "Okay?"

Hope nodded. She willed herself to relax against him. "I'm okay with that."

And then she realized it didn't take any will at all to turn her cheek to the strong beat of his heart. She didn't have to think twice about sliding her arms around his waist and drifting closer to the imprint of his harder hips and thighs against her body. Her breasts pillowed against the wall of Kevlar and man and she had no desire to run away from the comfort and strength he provided.

Pike's shoulders seemed to fold around her, blocking out the things that frightened her. He rubbed his chin against her hair and pressed a soft kiss to her temple. "You're not alone, Hope. It's you and me, remember? This guy's going to try to come after you, but he won't get to you, understand? I won't let him."

Whatever the reason behind this show of support, Hope curled her fingers into the back of his shirt and held on. She needed to feel safe for a few moments. She needed to know she'd made the right decision to agree to helping the police.

She needed to hear him say it again, in that deep, husky voice that danced across her eardrums and soothed the fear from her heart. "You're not alone."

Chapter Eight

"I don't like it." Pike squatted down in front of the shattered windowpane in the vestibule at the bridal shop. Hans was right there in his business, too, sniffing the broken glass littering the floor, whining in his throat as Pike pulled his flashlight from the back pocket of his jeans. Those dark brown eyes were trying to tell him something about what had happened here, but nothing beyond the signs of a routine break-in were making the dog's message any clearer. "What is it, boy?"

Hans sat and dipped his nose toward the corner where the frame around the busted pane met the adjoining brick wall. The dog's long black muzzle moved closer and closer to the dangerous shards of glass—a strong enough hit on something that Pike swung his light around and leaned in closer.

The nose never missed a trick. There was a stain of viscous red liquid clinging to an arrow point of glass protruding from the window frame. "Our guy cut himself."

Pike snapped a few pictures with his cell phone and texted them in with the report he'd made earlier. Then he patted the dog's flank and pushed to his feet, drawing the shepherd away from the crime scene. "Good boy." He bent down to ruffle up his fur before pulling the dog back into the shop. The intruder's injury probably wasn't the main reason he'd aborted the break-in. "You did good, Hansie. Bad Guy didn't get in. You did real good."

Hope was standing inside in the darkness of the closed shop, still wearing her trench coat and hugging her arms around her waist. "The one hour we were gone for pizza is when somebody breaks in? He's definitely watching the place."

"I know." Pike unhooked Hans's leash and harness and tossed him a crunchy treat from the pocket of the canvas jacket he wore. "I know it's what we were hoping for, but I hate to say it. Our man's taken the bait."

At her audible gasp, Pike reached over to flip on a light switch to flood the store with light and hopefully alleviate some of Hope's fear. Just as he'd imagined, she was pale as a ghost and keeping a wary eye on Hans to see where the dog settled down to enjoy his snack. But then those lake-gray eyes moved back to him, and he could see that, although she was rightfully concerned, she wasn't on the verge of wigging out on him as she had done in the past. "I did a quick walk-through while you two were outside. It doesn't look like anything has been taken or vandalized."

Not for the first time, he wondered exactly what had happened in her past to cause those panic attacks, and what it took for her to control them. He knew one thing, though, the woman was a fighter. Whatever he, KCPD, her father, those damn reporters or the Rose Red Rapist himself threw at her, she kept coming back for more. Pike never would have expected that kind of tenacity from such a shy, feminine woman. But he admired it. He liked it.

He was beginning to notice and appreciate a few too many things about the neighborhood spinster. Things that kept distracting him from the idea that this was an assignment he was working on, not his "let's be friends with everyone 'cause you got no game" love life.

But when he zeroed in on the patient expectation behind Hope's glasses, he remembered she was looking to him for protection and guidance through this undercover op, not another kissing lesson.

"Hans tracked the scent to the sidewalk across the street, but we lost the trail. The perp probably climbed into a vehicle and drove north. It'd be easy to get lost in city traffic if anyone did spot him." Pike shed his jacket and rolled up the sleeves of his chambray shirt, physically reminding himself that this was work. He propped open the door and took a closer look at the mess they'd come back to. Whatever the intruder had been after, he hadn't gotten through the newly replaced lock that led up to Hope's apartment, or through the second door that led into her shop. The most likely reason the perp had turned tail and run was stretched out on his belly and licking treat crumbs off the tile floor. "I'm guessing Hans scared him off. He's a better deterrent than your alarm system." He aimed the flashlight at the wire tacked to the molding beside the door. "Which looks like it's been cut. Camera's out, too."

"And we're sure it's him?" Her voice was closer now and he turned to find Hope standing in the shop doorway, holding a broom and dustpan, ready to keep moving forward. Definitely a fighter. But Pike had seen the worst the Rose Red Rapist and his accomplice could do. No matter how tenacious Hope might be, she didn't stand a chance on her own against them. Pike needed to make her understand that she was part of a team.

"Sorry." He took the broom and dustpan and set them just inside the door. "We'll have to wait for the CSIs to secure that blood sample, dust for prints and check for any other trace before we can clean up."

"Oh. Right." She plunged her hands inside the pockets of her coat, marked where Hans was lying and that the dog was stationary and headed over to the counter, where she pulled down a long ivory dress and carried it toward the fitting rooms. "Then I'll finish cleaning up in here while we wait."

Inhaling a deep breath, Pike resigned himself to his most difficult challenge yet, and followed her across the shop. "Hold up, Hope." He came up behind her in the mirror. He settled his hands lightly at her waist and looked at their reflection in the mirror. She hugged the simple, lacy dress in front of her and met his gaze in the mirror. He liked how the deep V of the neckline would reveal an enticing bit of skin, but the lace on top would keep her all covered up and ladylike. "You'd look beautiful in this."

A rosy hue of self-consciousness crept up her neck and warmed her cheeks. "Thank you." She blushed beautifully, without any false modesty, and he added that to the growing list of things he liked about this woman. He even kind of liked the rush he got, knowing something he said or did could cause all that pretty, porcelain skin to turn rosy. "Have you ever worn a tux?"

He nodded above her head. "Just once. My brother Alex's wedding."

"I bet you made a handsome figure all dressed up like that."

Pike chuckled. "Except for that noose of a tie and the shoes that pinched my feet, it wasn't altogether the worst wardrobe experience I've ever had."

"You're not a suit-and-tie kind of guy?"

Although he still wore his gun and badge on his belt, the jeans and work boots he wore now were pretty much the only uniform he had outside of his black KCPD regs. Unless he was truly off duty. Then it'd be running or fishing gear. "How'd you figure that out?"

Her lips softly pouted together when she smiled and something hitched inside him. Oh, yeah, he wouldn't mind a little more schooling in *that* department. But, tempting as it was to uncover a little more of the innocent passion hiding behind the spinster facade, Pike had something more important they needed to accomplish first.

"I think we need to have another lesson." He heard her breath catch when he reached around her to take the gown and drape it over the sofa.

"On what?"

"Trust. And what we can do to keep you safe."

She spun around with an apology stamped on her face. "I don't blame you for the attempted break-in. I know it takes me a little while to relax around new people, but I trust you."

Pike reached for her hand. "I need you to trust my partner, too."

Hope planted her feet and pulled against his grip. "I don't know if I'm comfortable—"

"Shh."

Hope's eyes widened like twin moons as he turned his head and whistled. Hans jumped to his feet and loped across the shop. His toenails clicked on the hard tile floor.

"Come on, boy. Up." Pike tapped his chest and the beast rose on his hind legs and propped two tawny paws on Pike's shoulders. He panted with excitement as Pike rubbed his hands along Hans's jowls and neck. "I always think he looks like he's smiling when I do that."

Sadly, the instant he'd released Hope's hand to pet the dog, Hope had darted away to hide behind the trio of mirrors. "Dogs don't smile."

"One step forward and two steps back, eh, buddy?" Pike's shoulders lifted with a deep breath. In a firmer tone, he pushed the dog down and ordered him to sit. Then he brushed off his hands and turned to Hope. "Come here. Hans is part of this undercover op, too, so we have to do this."

Hope couldn't seem to release her grip on the mirror. "Have to?"

"He won't hurt you. I promise." Pike held out his hand, asking her to trust him with this, too. He stretched his arm out farther. "He's part of your protection team, Hope. I need Hans to be able to do more than guard the place when we're gone. If, for some reason, I can't be there when you need me, Hans is my backup."

"Why wouldn't you be there…?" There was no blush on those pale cheeks now. "Oh."

He was her first line of defense. But he wasn't her only line of defense. "Hans doesn't know how to quit. If something happens to me, he'll protect you."

He waited patiently, never taking his eyes from hers. His patience paid off when she finally moved away from the mirror and laid her palm against his. He bit down on the urge to say, *Good girl,* and curled his fingers around hers to pull her up beside him, not two feet from the watchful eyes and black muzzle with all those teeth that seemed to terrify her.

Pike started talking before Hope's fear took hold and she ran from him again. "It's smart not to approach a dog you're unfamiliar with. But I know Hans and how he behaves. A dog's owner or handler should always clue you in on a dog's behavior before you jump in to pet him or play with him."

"That makes sense."

"Curl your fingers into a fist and let him sniff your scent before you try to touch him." Pike demonstrated what he wanted her to do. But when the dog's long red tongue slopped out over Pike's fist, Hope jumped back, digging her fingers into Pike's forearm as she ducked behind him. Hans's midnight-brown eyes shifted to her jerky movements and she retreated another step. But Pike pulled her right back to his side and the dog turned his attention back to him. "Most dogs bite because they're startled, not because they're inherently aggressive. Some breeds do attach their loyalty to one person or pack unit, and can be protective, but most of them will simply avoid or ignore an outsider unless you startle him or threaten his person or pack in some way."

Hope squeezed her hand more tightly around Pike's grip. "But some guard dogs *do* attack."

"If that's what they're trained to do. Unless he's got some mental defect, with enough time and consistency, and if they've been properly socialized, pretty much any dog can be trained to behave the way you want him to. So whether he's a safe dog or a danger to others usually depends on the owner." When she didn't respond, Pike leaned closer and nudged his shoulder against hers. "I'm thinking maybe you haven't been properly socialized, either."

A deep breath eased from Hope and she bumped him back, understanding he was teasing her. "Are you training me like the dog?"

"It's what I know how to do. Hans, *steh*." The dog lurched to his feet and Hope darted behind Pike. Her fingers clawed into the back of his shirt, and Pike's skin jumped where the ten needy imprints dug in. For a split second he was aware of breasts and grabbing hands and Hope's warm body clinging to his. But despite the instant, thumping urge that heated his blood, Pike made himself stand rock-still. He spoke to her in the same calm, articulate voice he'd used with the dog. "Now you tell him to lie down."

Her fingers tightened above his belt.

"Say his name and the command in a firm voice. You don't need to yell, just be succinct."

"He won't listen to me."

"The command is 'Hans, *platz.*'"

The big German shepherd tilted his head to one side, as though questioning who Pike was giving the command to. "Hans, *platz,*" Hope whispered into the back of his shirt.

Pike reached behind him and pulled Hope in front of him. "You'll have to say it so he can hear you."

The dog was looking up at her now. And though she backed that sweet, round bottom right against his groin, Pike resisted the urge to do more than cup Hope's shoulders and encourage her to try again.

"Hans. *Platz.*" Hope repeated the command in a stronger voice.

With what looked like a nod of his large, masked face, Hans stretched out on the floor at her feet. The warm vanilla scent of Hope's hair swept past Pike's nose when she tilted her head back to beam a smile at him. "He did it."

Pike squeezed her shoulders before moving to stand beside her. "Now reward him for obeying."

"How?"

"Treats. Playing a game—although I don't think

you're ready for tug-of-war quite yet." Pike squatted down beside Hope and mussed the dog's fur on top of his head. "Or pet him."

"I can't."

Pike tugged her down to her knees beside him. "You're the bravest woman I know, Hope. If you can stand up to the Rose Red Rapist, you can pet ol' Hansie here."

While she processed that reassurance, Pike placed her hand on top of Hans's head, and using his fingers to guide hers, showed Hope how to pet the warm, furry head.

"Easy." Stroke once. Again. "That's it. Did you know that petting a dog is supposed to lower your blood pressure?"

"I doubt they'd want to include me in that medical study." Despite the sarcasm, she took over the gentle massage, and Pike gradually pulled his hand away.

"He's warm like you," Hope observed, continuing the gentle strokes on her own. "Hairier, of course."

"I hope so."

"And his ears are so soft." Hope's grip on Pike's knee eased as she lengthened her strokes out to the dog's shoulder. Although Hans was panting lightly, he seemed to enjoy the tentative massage. "We had two dogs when I was little. Short-haired. Bigger than Hans." She swallowed hard and her fingers pinched his knee again. "Maybe because I was a little girl, they seemed bigger than they really were."

Was she opening up to him about whatever had triggered this phobia of dogs? Pike brushed a tawny curl away from Hope's cheek, silently urging her to continue. "What were their names?"

Pike felt the tension radiating off her. Hans sensed

it, too, judging by the whine in his throat. Her fingers twitched in Hans's fur. "Hank called them the baby-sitters."

His fingers stilled at her temple. Little girl. Big dogs. *Babysitters?* His gaze dropped to the scars on her wrist. He had a very bad feeling about where this conversation was going. "And?"

Her vision glazed over. Her hands clenched into fists. *Ah, hell.*

Sensing the change in the woman petting him, Hans raised his head, pushing his cold wet nose against Hope's arm. Pike saw curiosity, concern. But when Hans stretched his mouth open in a yawn, exposing those long rows of teeth, Hope saw something else.

"No, Jack!" She jerked back as a memory surfaced and terror consumed her. She tumbled into Pike, knocking him on his rear. "Stop!"

"Hope? What the…? Who's Jack? Hans, *bleib!*"

The dog froze, but Hope was moving. She pushed at Pike's shoulders, scrambling to her feet, fleeing toward the nearest door.

Pike got to his feet and grabbed her hand. "It's okay. You were doing great. Hans was liking it. That was a yawn. He's relaxing."

"I'm not." She swung around, punching at his wrist to free herself. "Let me go!"

"Hope?" Her eyes were wild, her skin flushed, her movements pure panic. "Hope!" She fisted her hand again. Enough. For both their sakes, Pike cinched his arms around hers like a straitjacket, lifting her off the floor, snugging her right up against his chest and pinning her while she shoved and twisted against him. Even though she lost one high heel, her kicking feet were still doing some damage. One caught Pike between the shins and tripped him onto the couch. Taking advantage of the opportunity, Pike rolled into the deep leather cushions, cocooning her thrashing body between his and the back of the couch. He put his lips against her ear and whispered her name. "Shh. Honey, you're all right. Hope? Hope."

"Stop it!" she yelled at whatever demon pursued her. "Please!" she wailed. Her running legs tangled with his. Her pounding hands fisted in his shirt. "Don't—"

Pike caught Hope's face between his hands and closed his mouth over hers. Something desperate, something clever and maybe something completely selfish had flashed through him as her fear turned into sobs. He wasted no time with a patient tutorial. He forced her lips apart and plunged inside—giving, taking, demanding. The initial shock of the kiss snapped her out of the panic and stilled her struggles.

Hope's deep gray eyes opened and locked onto his. His breath steamed through his nose as he lifted his mouth to ensure that she was back in the present. Here. With him. Not afraid.

In the next breath, a very different sort of urgency erupted between them. Hope wound her arms around Pike's neck and pulled him back into the kiss. Her chest and hips slid against his, seeking the full body contact he'd forced on her moments earlier.

Pike thrust his tongue inside her hot, open mouth, drinking in her eager welcome. He palmed her butt and twisted them to a more comfortable position on the couch, with her lying partly beneath him, giving his hands easier access to discover all the secrets of her lush, womanly body. While her lips skidded across his jaw, sampling a taste here, experimenting with a nip there, Pike freed the rest of her hair from its confining clip and sifted the silky tresses through his greedy fingers.

"What should I do?" she whispered in a moist, breathy caress against his neck that sent an electric current straight down to the south side of his belt buckle. She closed her teeth gently around his earlobe and Pike groaned at the delicate maneuver that was somehow shy and bold at the same time. "Is that okay?"

"Oh, yeah, honey." He kissed her lips again, praised her, thanked her. "Told you you were a natural."

While her fingers roamed curiously across his shoulders and chest, Pike worked his gun from its holster and set it safely on the floor beside them. He went back to remove her glasses, and her eyes widened like beautiful lakes warmed by the stars. "You're liking this, too, right? I mean you'd tell me if—"

He silenced the foolish protest with another kiss, telling her with his lips and hands and hardening body just how much he was liking what she was doing to him. Pike hoped to God she knew the difference between those intimacies they'd done for show and the serious reality that was happening between them right now.

Any sampling of her shy kisses, any suspicion about her hidden curves and beauty, was coming to life and going far beyond his expectations with each needy grab of her hands, each stroke of her tongue that grew bolder and bolder against his, each soft groan of pleasure that hummed in her throat. His pulse thundered in his ears. His fingers burned to discover every inch of her. He was a thirsty man, getting drunk on the finest whiskey that no other man had been privileged enough to taste.

He vaguely remembered the panic that had set them on this course—the dog, the break-in, the tension that must have been simmering between them for months. There was only now. Here. Hope.

And it wasn't enough. Sliding his hands down between them, Pike loosened the belt and buttons of her coat and pushed it open. He smiled against her mouth as he met the soft wool of her suit jacket. He unhooked that belt and worked the buttons free. Her fingers were in his hair as he uncovered the layer of cotton blouse. Pike moaned his frustration and stole another kiss before resolutely attacking the buttons there. And then he was sliding his hand inside and palming one of those full, beautiful breasts. He squeezed at the silk and lace covering it until it poked to attention and drew his lips toward the tempting peak.

"You're so pretty, Hope." She gasped when he closed his mouth over the pebbled nipple, wetting it through the slip and bra she wore. "So, so pretty."

She arched against him, then quickly drew back, no doubt discovering the eager bulge behind his zipper. "I don't know what… I can't even think. I want…"

"It's okay, honey. You can touch me." Her instincts were good. She'd already unbuttoned his shirt and slipped her hand inside to brand his skin. "Do whatever you want. Or if this is going too fast, we'll stop right now.

"But you…" Her hand drifted down his side and cupped his hip. A few inches closer and she could finish him with a hand job. Pike groaned in anticipation but held himself still. He wouldn't push her. He wouldn't do anything that might frighten Hope and spoil this perfect moment. "You're…" Her face colored a beautiful shade of pink. "…ready."

Oh, man, was that an understatement! But there was

something equally important going on here. That trust he'd always wanted from her was growing stronger.

"I won't break, remember?" He tunneled his fingers into her hair again, loving how dusky and pretty her eyes looked up close like this. "I can stop. You're driving me crazy, but the timing's not right. Not yet," he promised, in case she was thinking, for one naive moment, that he didn't want her with every fiber of his being. He gathered the blouse and suit and coat together and pulled them over her. "Not yet."

Her fingers fumbled at the buttons of his shirt, trying to do her part to ease the throttle back a couple of notches between them, but failing miserably. "I'm driving *you* crazy?"

He laughed at the incredulous statement coming from those delectable, kiss-stung lips. "My brother says I haven't got any game when it comes to women. I'm better with dogs and fish and my hunting rifle." He caught her hand and stilled the distracting fingers against his chest. "But you, Miss Thing, are a real talent."

"Your brother's wrong." The knot furrowing between her eyebrows told him Hope was dead serious with that compliment, and Pike leaned in to kiss the worry spot. "You can be very charming," she insisted.

Maybe to a thirty-two-year-old virgin with panic attacks and trust issues who was just now discovering her sexuality.

But Pike's grin faded when a telephone rang.

"Is that yours or mine?" Hope patted her clothes, but with her trench coat and jacket tangled between them, she was having trouble even locating her pockets as the phone rang again. "It's mine."

Pike was content to cuddle and hold on to the connection beyond their task force mission he and Hope had just made. "Let it go."

"At this hour?" Her cheeks were flushed again, and she was pushing at his chest and the couch behind her, struggling to sit up. "It's my life intruding. My stupid past keeps trying to ruin any chance I have at a future."

He felt the vibration of her phone against his thigh and eased out a weary sigh. The moment that had just happened between them was gone. Forgetting his own discomfort, he swung his feet to the floor and sat up. "What does that mean?"

She shot to her feet as the phone rang a fourth time. "Someday, Pike, you'll find out what a sad, screwed-up life I have."

"Had," he corrected, pulling her phone from her coat pocket and handing it to her before she could find it. "There's nothing wrong with you."

She answered on the fifth ring. "Damn it, Hank! Leave me alone—"

Hope's entire body went suddenly and utterly still.

Pike was on his feet in an instant, sliding an arm behind her waist and lowering his ear to listen to the mechanically disguised voice on the line. "Who's Hank?" The tinny voice laughed. "And here I thought you were a good girl. You're an opportunistic slut, just like the rest of them." There was an ominous pause. "You be careful."

When a click ended the call, Hope collapsed against him. "Pike?"

"Get in the dressing rooms and stay out of sight." He took the phone from her and tucked it into her pocket before shutting her inside. Then he scooped up his gun from the floor and ran to kill the lights, check the doors and peer through the windows to account for every car, pedestrian and window with potential eyes on Hope's shop.

He saw nothing suspicious, no one showing more interest in Fairy Tale Bridal than they should. But he could feel it in his bones that that pervert had been watching them on the couch, that he was watching the place right now—that he'd taken a shy woman's hard-won sense of confidence and composure and shaken it right down to the ground.

Pike glanced back at the long leather couch, feeling a little shaken himself at how fast and how far Hope Lockhart had gotten under his skin. But he made the man recede and the cop in him take over. Finishing the sweep, he holstered his weapon and pulled out his cell to call the task force leader.

The senior detective picked up on the first ring. "Yes?"

"Montgomery? Pike Taylor." Hearing the noise of precinct HQ in the background, Pike checked his watch. It was just after eleven o'clock. Didn't the guy ever sleep? Pike wasn't sure he could now. "He's on the hook. He's coming for her." No need to clarify the unsub they were talking about. "He just called and threatened Hope."

"I'll notify the others. Nick and Annie are already en route to process the scene. I'll be there ASAP."

"No. You can't send in the cavalry yet. Remember? Too big of a police presence may scare this guy off. Let's just address the break-in with a routine response."

"But if that blood you mentioned matches the DNA in our system—"

"It'll match. It's his. I know it is."

"Then let me send—"

"No. The guy is long gone. Hans can track him by scent now, and he's not here."

"Are you sure you don't want more backup?"

"I'm sure. I'm not putting Hope through this for nothing. If he goes underground and we don't catch this guy now, she'll never be able to stop looking over her shoulder."

"How's she holding up?"

"Like a champ, given the circumstances." Pike's long strides carried him quickly back to the dressing rooms. He trailed his fingers along the smooth leather on the back of the couch, slowing his steps, then stopping—processing what his instincts were trying to tell him. With the height and angle of that couch, the perp shouldn't have been able to see anything from the street or parking lot once he and Hope had stretched out together. Either the two of them making out was a lucky assumption on the caller's part, or...

"Make sure Annie brings something to sweep for hidden cameras, too. We may have a spy right here in the shop." Pike thought about the funny little guy who'd been flirting with Hope that first day. He turned toward the flower shop across the street where the guy worked. What was his name? Leon? Hope said he'd been doing odd jobs around here for months. How easy would it have been for him to hide a camera in here? Pike raised his gaze to the ceiling above him. Would Leon have access to Hope's apartment, too?

Hope was waiting anxiously for him at the dressing room door as soon as he pushed it open. Her clothes were rebuttoned, cinched up tight. But she'd lost the clip for her hair, and the long curls fanned around her shoulders, leaving Pike with the impression she didn't have all her protective emotional armor back in place yet, either. "Is help coming?" she asked.

Pike reached for her hand and she squeezed both of hers around his. "Don't send any backup," Pike repeated, for Hope's understanding as well as the detective's. "Not yet. He's taken the bait, but he's not in our trap yet."

"Roger that." As irritated as Spencer Montgomery sounded at being ordered by a younger officer to stay away from a crime scene, the senior detective let Pike take point on this. "We'll keep our distance. But call for backup the instant you need us. In the meantime, do your job, Taylor."

That went without saying.

"Yes, sir. Hans, *pass auf!*" Holding hands wasn't good enough. He verified Hans was standing guard at the door before pulling Hope into his chest and wrapping his arm around her. Her arms snaked around his waist to hold on and he pressed a kiss to the crown of her hair. "We'll keep her safe."

Chapter Nine

Hope would never have imagined that she could be afraid inside a church. Nor would she ever have expected to see Pike Taylor being afraid of anything besides sticking his oversize foot in his mouth.

But he'd been reluctant to let her leave the shop after lunch. *"There won't be anyone around to keep an eye on you,"* he'd argued.

"No," she'd gently corrected him. *"You and Hans won't be there to protect me. But I won't be alone."*

And she wasn't. Hope had her bride-to-be client, the client's mother, the minister, her friend Robin Lonergan to consult on floral arrangements and Leon Hundley, one of Robin's employees, at the church with her.

The planning meeting for the client's summer wedding was going smoothly. Everyone had shown up on time. There'd been no strange requests and the autumn sun outside was bright enough to illuminate the interior of the spacious sanctuary without turning on any lights.

And yet Hope couldn't shake the idea that there was someone else here with them—someone moving through the denuded trees and orange-red shrubs swaying in the breeze outside the church windows, peeking in, or clinging to the shadows in the farthest corners of the building where the sunlight couldn't reach.

Hope startled when a branch scraped against the window near the end of the pew where she was sitting. And even though she should be taking notes about what floral displays the church would allow in the sanctuary, her attention fixed on the movement outside until she saw the mourning dove that had landed in the tree and shaken the branch suddenly take flight again.

Her brave words from that morning might come back to haunt her. Even with the German shepherd beside him, a tall, rugged cop on the premises right about now would go a long way toward dispelling this anxiety that fueled her imagination. *"Just like you told Detective Montgomery. I can't have cops around me all the time, or we'll scare this guy off. And you have to patrol the neighborhood like you do every other day or he might suspect we're up to something. Try not to worry, Pike. I'll be surrounded by people the entire time I'm gone, or I'll be in my car."*

"Try not to worry, she says." Pike had reached into her coat pocket and pulled out her phone. He punched in his number and put the phone back in her hands. *"Call me when you leave the church and come straight home. I'll meet you here. And if you sense anything hinky while you're away from me, call. Push one number and I'll answer."*

She'd nodded, touched by his concern. Then he'd palmed the back of her neck and pulled her onto her toes to plant a hard, quick, very personal kiss on her mouth. And there hadn't even been an audience except for the omnipresent dog.

"I'll be here." And he had been until she'd given

directions to her assistant running the shop, and had driven away.

Hope could still feel that kiss. The same way she could still feel the arousing heat of his hands moving over her body from the night before, and remember how uniquely different and altogether exciting the hardness of his long, lean body had felt beneath her exploring hands.

She was learning just how seriously the man took his job, and she truly believed she couldn't have been assigned a more skilled and dedicated protector. She could even understand the logic behind his repeated efforts to help her get along with Hans.

So where did that make-out session on the couch last night fit in? Even she wasn't so naive to think that had been part of their undercover charade. But was the passion that had flared between them just a case of convenience? A man got horny and she got curious enough to test the simmering sexual needs she'd kept buried inside her for far too long? Or was there something more tender, more caring evolving out of the friendship she and Edison Pike Taylor were forging between them?

Another flurry of movement, from the center aisle of the church this time, stirred Hope from her thoughts. Their meeting was breaking up. People were leaving. With one more glance toward the window, she stood to say goodbye to her clients and assure them she had their next appointment in her planner.

While the minister walked the two women out, Robin summoned her assistant from the back of the church. "Leon, would you take those sample arrangements back to the van while we finish up the paperwork?"

"Yes, ma'am." Leon strolled to the front of the church

and started packing the decorative arrangements into boxes and stacking them up on a dolly.

Robin tucked her short dark hair behind her ears before carrying a spray of silk carnations up to the altar to set them into one of the boxes before Leon finished up. "Oh, and my husband and daughter are coming to pick me up here, so you can head on back to the shop. I know you worked over lunch to help me set up here, so unless Shirley has any new deliveries that need to go out, go ahead and take the rest of the evening off."

"Will do." Leon closed the top box and pulled his uniform cap from his hip pocket. "Thanks, Ms. Carter." His neck reddened above the collar of the green company shirt he wore. "Er, I mean Mrs. Lonergan."

"That's okay, Leon," Robin assured him. "I'm still getting used to the name change myself."

"Yes, ma'am." He settled the green cap over his short dark hair and winked to Hope. "See you later."

"Okay." She smiled back and then gathered her notebook and color cards and dropped them into her tote bag.

"You were a million miles away." Robin waited at the end of the pew for Hope to join her.

"I wish. Sorry if I got distracted at the end there. I got stuck inside my head, overthinking things."

Robin linked her arm through Hope's as they followed Leon out. "What are you worried about? Surely not this wedding?"

"Not at all." At the task force's request, to ensure that the truth of what they were doing wouldn't accidentally get out, Hope hadn't been allowed to share the details of their operation with even her best friend. But Robin had to know there'd been some big changes in Hope's life recently. Surely, it wouldn't hurt to share a little of why she was so distracted these days. "Someone broke into my shop last night. Disabled the alarm system and the camera."

"Oh, my gosh. Are you okay? Was anything stolen?"

"I'm fine."

"You should have told me."

Hope grinned as she pushed open the front door of the church and headed down the concrete steps to the parking lot. "Oh, right. I've been a third wheel my whole life, Robin. You and Jake haven't even been married a month. Like I'm going to be the one to interrupt your honeymoon." She squeezed Robin's arm, letting her know she didn't feel slighted in the least by her friend's preoccupation with her new husband and adopted daughter. "Besides, I think the dog on the premises scared the intruder away."

"That's right. The scenery at your shop has changed recently. Officer Taylor sure has been hanging around a lot." Robin hugged her arm tighter, leaning in with a shamelessly nosy question. "Is he as scary as you thought he was? What's he like?"

"Blunt. He likes to tease." Hope felt the warmth creep into her cheeks at her next thought. "And he's a really good kisser. Of course, I don't have all that much experience—"

"That's okay. You know what you like and you like how he does it? Then he's a great kisser. I'm so happy for you. I knew if the right guy came along, he'd see you for the treasure you are."

After their first introduction at a neighborhood business development meeting three years earlier, Robin had quickly become Hope's dearest friend and confidante. She hated lying to her about her relationship with

Pike. "I guess I kind of figured I'd be growing old by myself. My feelings for Pike have really surprised me."

That part, at least, wasn't a lie.

"Trust your instincts, Hope. Trust your heart. Sometimes love comes at us in unexpected ways, from unexpected places." Robin turned her attention to the big brawny man unfolding himself from behind the wheel of the extended-cab pickup that had just pulled in. Jake Lonergan's less than handsome face reminded Hope of the thugs who terrorized the good guys in any of a dozen movies she could name. But he'd proved hero enough a few months earlier when Robin and her infant daughter's life were in danger. "You might be surprised at just how happy you can be."

"Ladies." Even a smile did little to change the harsh contours of Jake's scarred-up face, but there was nothing but adoration shining from his pale eyes as he leaned in to kiss Robin and take her bag for her. "Emma's asleep in her car seat, so I'll leave the truck running." Hope smiled as he leaned over to drop a kiss on her cheek, too. "Did Robin tell you that Emma's on the verge of crawling now? She's got scooting across the floor on her bottom mastered, but I know she's going to roll over and take off any day now."

Jake looked less like an infant girl's father than anyone Hope could imagine, yet she'd never seen a man take to daddyhood the way the former DEA agent had. "Do you have any new pictures?"

"A few."

"Liar." Robin gave him a nudge toward the truck to load her things. "He's taken hundreds."

Jake shrugged, unable to deny his guilt. "'Bye, Hope."

"'Bye, Jake."

Robin wrapped her arms around Hope and squeezed her in a goodbye hug. "I swear that man would put a crown on Emma's head if her neck could support it."

Hope hugged her back. "Jake is a wonderful father." Just like one she would have wished for growing up. "Emma's lucky."

"She wouldn't be with us now if Jake hadn't been around." Robin's loving smile flatlined and she had a serious, sisterly word for Hope. "You make sure you stay safe, too. With everything that's happened in our neighborhood? Now to hear you've been broken into?"

"I'm fine. Really."

"Well, don't hesitate to call us if you need anything. Anytime of day or night."

"I won't."

Robin's smile was back. "And we're going to have you and Officer Taylor out to the house sometime for dinner."

"Oh, that's not—" Hope reminded herself to smile and keep the charade of her relationship with Jake as real as she could make it. Dinner with friends would be a normal couple thing, wouldn't it? "Okay. Talk to you soon."

Hope said goodbye and loaded her things into the backseat of her car before climbing in behind the wheel. She'd just pulled her keys from her pocket purse when a sharp rap on her window startled her. With a shrieking gasp, she dropped her keys to the floor.

"Leon." She muttered his name with an apology, picked up her keys and started the car before rolling down the window. "Yes?"

Leon hunched into the open window, pulled his cap into his hands and smiled. "Yeah, um, I was just wondering if you had plans for tonight. Since the boss is letting me go early, I thought we could get a bite to eat somewhere, or something."

Really? They'd known each other for two years, and he'd picked today to ask her out? Hope forced her gaping mouth to close. Even without the charade of a fiancé to maintain, she wasn't interested in a date. "I can't."

Leon thumped the side of her door and straightened. And then he was leaning into the window again. "It's him, isn't it? I knew I'd lost you."

Lost her? Had he been under the impression that she was ever his to lose? "You and I have barely spoken about anything except repairs at my shop and our jobs. We're friends. But that's all we'll ever be."

His brown eyes narrowed into slits that made her lean away from the window. "After I did all those things for you, like fixing your door. I would have come and sprayed for bugs or set traps for you, too, just so you wouldn't have to dirty your hands."

Bugs? Traps? As in mouse traps?

"You sent those awful gifts?" Hope gripped the wheel and stopped retreating. She'd been grossed out, confused and terrified by the creepy bugs and dead rodent—and by the knowledge that whoever had left them must have been watching her shop and apartment very closely. This didn't make any logical sense. "You've been sabotaging things at my shop as an excuse to come over and spend time with me? What, so you could save the day and be my hero? I thought you were being a nice friend. I offered to pay you for your time." Her stomach got a little queasy at the twisted means of courtship. "Those gifts frightened me."

He reached into the car and curled his fingers over hers on the steering wheel. "I just wanted you to need me the way I need you. You would never talk to me, so I had to make up a reason for you to come out of your shell."

And she thought she'd been backward about meeting someone and developing a relationship. She slid her hand from beneath his and articulated the truth as succinctly as she knew how. "Leon, I don't feel the same way about you. I'm sorry." Confusion moved through disgust and went straight to anger. "You broke into my shop last night, didn't you? You made that phone call?"

He plunked his cap back on his thin brown hair. "What are you talking about?"

"Did you break in the window to my shop and cut the alarm wire? Did you spray-paint over the security camera? Pike's dog could have killed you if you'd gotten all the way inside."

"Oh, so now everything that goes wrong in your life is my fault? I suppose you're going to report me to that cop you've been shackin' up—"

"Did you break in?"

"No! I was at my mother's last night."

"And you didn't call and threaten me?" Hope's indignation waned as other, more disturbing, possibilities ran through her head. If Leon hadn't installed the tiny camera Pike's friend, Annie Hermann, had found hidden inside a light at her shop, then who had? The list of suspects who'd have that kind of access to her shop was short. The list of anyone interested enough in her life and business to go to that kind of trouble was even shorter.

"Hundley." Jake Lonergan's massive shadow fell over Leon, and the short man with a sick idea of romance froze for a second before taking a step away from Hope's car. "You've got some deliveries to make for my wife, don't you?"

"You're not my boss, Mr. Lonergan."

Jake crossed his arms over the front of the form-fitting black sweater he wore. With that heavyweight boxer's body and scarred-up face, Jake Lonergan in intimidation mode was scary enough to make Hope shrink away, even though he was defending her. "If my wife tells you to do something, you do it. Understood?"

With Jake daring the much smaller man to argue with him, Leon quickly gave up the fight. "See you around, Hope," he said, sneering. "If anything else goes wrong at your shop, you get someone else to fix it."

"I will." He scurried away to the flower shop van, sparing one contemptuous glare toward Hope before shifting into gear and speeding out of the parking lot.

She was still running through a list of names of men who had access to her shop when Jake braced his hands at the open window of her car. "There's something about that little weasel I've never liked. Call your boyfriend. Tell him you're on your way. Robin and I will wait until you leave."

Boyfriend. Right. The undercover ruse was working if both creepy Leon and her true friends believed she and Pike were a couple. Wishing more than she should that her time with Pike Taylor wasn't a lie, Hope looked up and smiled. "Thanks, Jake."

Robin and Jake followed her out to the highway before turning off to their home in the country outside the K.C. area. Hope waved them a thanks and continued toward downtown.

As the miles passed, she was torn between simmering resentment at the unnecessary fear Leon had caused her, and a fear that ran much colder, much deeper, when she thought about someone even more devious, more dangerous stalking her. Leon's misguided efforts would have provided the Rose Red Rapist a perfect misdirection to throw the police off their ability to track down his movements and his threats against Hope. He could have been watching her from that very first night she'd spotted his van.

Could the lights reflecting in her apartment, and the movements in the shadows around her, be attributed to Leon Hundley? Or were Leon's crude attempts to work his way into her life a convenient distraction for the police while a more secretive threat watched her from unseen vantage points and hidden cameras? Maybe Leon was a really, really good liar—and her would-be suitor and the serial rapist were the same man. The one thing she was certain of was that she needed to get home to Pike and tell him about Leon's disquieting confession.

Hope rounded a wide turn on the interstate to head south toward the city, and found herself veering a bit into the passing lane. She tapped on the brake to turn off the cruise control. Although the light on the dash blinked off, centrifugal force was still making her lean toward the door. "Slow down, already."

She tapped on the brake without detecting any change on the speedometer. If anything, as the straight stretch of highway dropped into a valley, she was picking up speed. "Really?"

The third time she pushed, the pedal went all the way to the floor and she went faster yet.

"Oh, my God."

She had no brakes.

Panic bubbled up in her throat, but she swallowed it down and gripped the wheel harder, judging the thankfully empty stretch of road, the brown grass median to her left and the trees climbing the steep hill to her right. She tapped on the useless pedal again. "What do I do?"

Turn off the engine? Then she'd have no steering. Shift to a lower gear? Not at this speed!

"Call me. I'll be here."

Hope risked taking her hand off the wheel to pull her cell phone from her coat and punch in Pike's number. She'd clicked it to speakerphone and dropped it onto the seat beside when Pike picked up. "Hope?"

She put both hands on the steering wheel again and raised her voice so he could hear her. "Something's wrong with my car. I can't slow down."

She pitched forward when she hit the bottom of the valley and raced up the next incline at breakneck speed. "Pike?"

"Where are you?" She could hear hurried footsteps and measured breathing. Pike was running.

She gave him the highway number and closest exit she remembered passing. "I'm heading up a hill now. I'm losing some speed, but not much yet. I'll try to pull off. But if I reach the other side—"

He muttered one swift, succinct swearword, then started giving orders. "Put on your blinkers and make sure you're buckled in. I'm calling highway patrol right now. Listen to me. Pump your brakes. Sometimes you can rebuild the pressure." He went through a list of things to try to compensate for the damaged brakes.

But none of them were going to do her any good.

Hope's eyes went to the rearview mirror, and her breath locked up in her chest.

A white van crested the hill behind her, rapidly closing the distance between them.

"Pike?"

"I'm on my way."

He'd be too late.

HOPE'S HAND TIGHTENED around Pike's. "Wait."

Ignoring the audience of waiting patients, visitors and staff in the east lobby of the Truman Medical Center, Pike stopped the nurse pushing Hope's wheelchair toward the exit and knelt beside her. He knew it wasn't the crowd inside that made her nervous, but the onslaught of cameras and reporters waiting in the parking lot outside that put the shadows of fear into her eyes. Pike brushed a curling lock of hair away from the deep purple bruise on her forehead. "You say the word and I'll get you out of here through some back hallway or employee exit. You just spent a night in the hospital. You don't have to talk to these people."

She adjusted her glasses at her temple, and for several tense moments, those beautiful eyes looked straight into Pike's soul and tried to tell him something. But then she blinked and the message was hidden behind the dutiful tilt of her gaze up to Detective Montgomery, who stood on the other side of her chair.

Hope's grip pulsed around Pike's, and her pale lips smiled. "Yes, I do. I know what I'm supposed to say. I just need a second to gather my thoughts and steel my nerves. That's the whole point of this, isn't it? Using me to bait the trap? We wanted his attention focused on me so he'd come after me. I won't give up now."

"The bastard tried to kill you."

"He didn't succeed." But the burn on her forearm from the air bag, the bruising from her seat belt and the bumps and scrapes over the rest of her body told him the outcome of sailing over a ditch and flying up a brushy hillside to finally wedge her car between two trees could have had a very different outcome. "The truck driver who stopped to help me said he saw a man running to a white van parked on the shoulder of the road when he pulled up. The trucker must have scared him away before he could get to my car and…"

Finish the job. Pike nodded. He'd been there when the EMTs had pulled a dazed and bleeding Hope from the wreck. "Remind me to give that guy a medal."

"Pike?" Hope's gentle fingers brushed across his rough jaw, reminding him he still needed a fresh uniform and a shave after his vigil in the chair beside her hospital bed. Why was she smiling at him? After all KCPD and the Rose Red Rapist were putting her through, how could she still be brave enough to smile? "It's not the first time I've been afraid of something and did it anyway because I had to. I may not be a firecracker on the outside, but I can be tough when I really need to be."

The old scars Pike had seen along her shoulder, wrist and collarbone each time a nurse had come to check on Hope's progress through the night made him think this wasn't the first time she'd cheated death. They also made him seethe with something akin to a protective rage when he thought of her father and her fear of dogs and how they all must tie into that painful childhood and grown-up panic attacks she didn't like to talk about.

The woman shouldn't have to keep fighting for survival. Pike tilted his head to the astutely patient detective eavesdropping on their conversation. "Montgomery, help me out."

But it was Hope who answered. "Pike." With another gentle touch, she turned his gaze back to hers. "I have to do this. Just promise you'll stay with me."

He nodded. Yes. Screw the charade. He wasn't leaving her to patrol his beat or attend a task force briefing. He wasn't going to family dinners or football games with his brothers. He was staying right by her side until that slimy, cowardly cockroach of a man who'd done this to her was in jail and could no longer hurt her.

Hope inhaled a deep breath. "Okay. I'm ready."

Pike pulled her fingers to his lips and kissed them before rising and taking the nurse's place behind the wheelchair. "Let's get it over with."

Hope's friend Robin had brought jeans, a sweater and a flannel-lined knock-around coat for Hope to wear home. Yet Pike could feel her shivering in the afternoon sun the moment the first light flashed and the barrage of questions started. With Spencer Montgomery, Nick Fensom and Kate Kilpatrick keeping the reporters at a barely respectful distance, Pike pushed the chair out to the far curb and bit his tongue while the press had at her.

Vanessa Owen pushed to the front of the pack, urging her cameraman in beside her to get a shot of Hope's bruises and bandages. "You claim the Rose Red Rapist ran you off the highway."

Hope squinted against the bright light. "I know it was him."

"You saw his face? You were careening down the interstate at eighty miles an hour and you took the time to look at the driver's face?"

"I wasn't going that fast. I was already having car trouble. I'd slowed down."

Gabriel Knight was there, too, with his notepad and cynical voice. "That unpopulated stretch of highway north of the city where your car broke down is pretty far from the Rose Red Rapist's usual hunting ground."

"He must have planned it." Her chest rose and fell more rapidly as her breathing quickened. "The police found brake fluid at a church where I was attending a business meeting. They believe my car was sabotaged."

"Are you sure you're not just a bad driver, Miss Lockhart?"

Her knuckles were turning white on the arms of the wheelchair. "His van clipped my bumper, sending me into the ditch. I'm lucky I didn't roll my car."

"Forget the accident, Gabe. What did he look like?" Vanessa Owen took center stage again. "You say you saw the Rose Red Rapist. You're certain it's the same man you identified last weekend, near where LaDonna Chambers was found raped and murdered?"

"Yes."

"What did he look like?"

Pike stepped in when the brunette's microphone got too close to Hope. "Enough. The woman could have died. Cut her a break."

"What about the other women who died, Officer? Don't their families deserve to know who this man is? Don't the rest of us have a right to know from whom we should protect ourselves?" With a smile that was more shark than serene, the reporter retreated a step. "Miss Lockhart, give us something. Was he tall? Short? White? Black? Dark-haired? Blond?"

"A white man." Hope's voice sounded small.

"How old was he?"

"I…" She lowered her head, tilting only her eyes toward the camera. "He wore a surgical mask."

"So you didn't see his face."

Her chest heaved with a deep breath. "I saw enough."

"What color were his eyes?"

"Did he say anything to you?"

She twisted her fingers in her lap. "He didn't speak."

"Did he touch you?"

Her head shot up. "He tried to kill me. He walked up

to my car…after it crashed. He… I heard him coming through the brush… I tried to get out, but…"

Pike could see the panic stirring in Hope's pale skin and trembling mouth. If she hadn't run out of patience yet, he had. Ignoring the cameras, the questions and his superior officer, Pike scooped Hope into his arms and lifted her from the chair. "She's done answering questions."

"Miss Lockhart!"

As soon as Hope curled her fingers into his collar and laid her head against his shoulder, Pike carried her across the driveway to his truck.

Kate Kilpatrick took over the press conference and diverted most of the reporters' attention to her. "Please. Miss Lockhart's car was totaled. She's lucky to be alive. She needs her rest."

"Can *you* give us a description?"

Dr. Kate's voice faded in the distance. "For obvious reasons, the police don't want to give away all the details of these crimes. But we are looking for a white male, late twenties to forty—"

"I can walk." Hope's lips moved against Pike's neck in a weary protest, but he just held on tighter. He didn't set her on her feet until they reached the black-and-white K-9 truck. And even then, it was just long enough to get the door unlocked and open before he lifted her onto the passenger seat. "Where's the beast?" she asked, looking into the backseat.

Pike reached across her lap to fasten the seat belt. "My brother Alex took Hans for the night. He'll drop him off at your apartment once we get there."

With Hans gone, what fight she had left seemed to drain right out of her. "I hope that was enough. I tried." She squeezed her eyes shut and turned away from the crowd.

"You did great." He pulled a stadium blanket from under the seat and covered her up. "I'll get you home, Hope. Just as fast as I humanly can." He smoothed her hair off her face and earned a nod of appreciation, or maybe just understanding, before Pike closed the door and hurried around the hood.

A stern-faced Spencer Montgomery stopped him in his tracks. Pike pulled up to his superior height, irritated by protocol and unspoken accusations and his own guilt. "Detective?"

Spencer Montgomery couldn't be intimidated. He pulled back the edges of his jacket and propped his hands at his waist. "Don't mess this up, Taylor. We need our perp to think she knows exactly who we're after."

"She said enough."

"Are you getting emotionally attached to this woman?"

"Yes, sir."

"Yes, sir, you won't blow this sting operation, or yes, sir, you have feelings for her?"

The promise of the coming winter chilled the late-morning air. But there was something as warm and certain as it was unfamiliar filling Pike's chest when he looked inside the truck to see Hope huddling beneath the blanket. He nudged aside the detective before opening his door and climbing in beside her. "Both."

Chapter Ten

The cut on his forearm stung like the annoyance Hope Lockhart had turned out to be. He tossed back the whiskey in his glass and poured himself another while the woman who'd doctored his wound sat on the edge of the bed, towel-drying her hair.

"Be a love and pour me one of those, will you?" she asked.

For several seconds, he stood at the drink cart, his hand fisting around his glass so tightly it should have cracked. He drank that shot down, too, needing the sharp burn of the liquid to cut through the anger stirring in his blood and poisoning his thoughts. When he could think again, he poured himself a third whiskey, and filled a glass for her before taking the drink to her.

"I told you to let me handle it." He nodded toward the television they'd just turned off. "Now it's all over the news. Hope Lockhart is talking."

With a smile that was as smug as it was seductive, she clinked her glass against his, then drank the whole thing down like a man. "I've given you the perfect alibi, taking the van out to north Kansas City for you while you were here in town. You should be grateful."

Grateful? To a woman?

He took the glass she handed him back to the cart. He tried to simply set it down, but couldn't help himself. There were maids to do this kind of thing, but he picked up both glasses and carried them into the bathroom, where he washed them in the sink, removing saliva and fingerprints and any other contaminant that might linger. He dried them with a towel until they sparkled, lined them up, just so, on the counter, then washed and dried his hands until they were pink and chapped and just as clean.

He pulled a bottle of vinegar from his toiletry bag and poured the liquid over his hands, sterilizing them before rinsing again. Then he dabbed on enough cologne to mask the tangy scent and returned the glasses to the drink cart.

He might be a sick man. But he wasn't a foolish one. "I don't like that you made the decision without me. I've been keeping a close eye on Hope. I don't think she knows as much as the police claim."

"Didn't you hear her at that press conference?" The robe the woman wore barely covered the curves of her body as she stood and sauntered across the room to him. This woman tempted him. Repulsed him. She was good at her job and good for him, and he hated that he needed her. She'd hurt him deeply, yet he couldn't walk away. He owed her far too much and she knew him far too well. "She saw your surgical mask."

"Because you wore one today."

"Because she saw you that night. I never got that close to her car, or she'd be dead by now." She touched her fingers to his jaw, and his skin crawled, even though he knew she'd just come from the shower. "She knows the color of your skin. She may know more, but she's too broken to share it."

"You think Hope is lying?"

She pulled the towel from her hair and tossed it onto the bed. "You obviously do, too, or you wouldn't be spying on her."

"Then why hasn't she called me out? She knows me."

"She's afraid of you." She combed her fingers through her hair and shook the dark layers behind her back in a move that was probably meant to entice. But all he saw was the damp wad of towel soiling his bed. "I've looked her in the eye, just like you. That woman's afraid of her own shadow."

"Then we have nothing to worry about."

She faced him, backing up that beauty with cold, hard logic. "We have everything to worry about. Haven't you ever read fairy tales? The ugly duckling turns into a swan. The poor little ash girl becomes a princess. She'll change. She'll snap out of this stupor she's in. She'll come up against something or someone she fears even more than you. It may not be today or tomorrow, but one day, she'll name you for the ogre of the story you are."

"Ogre?"

The bitch smiled. "How many women have you raped? You're not exactly hero material, are you?"

"And you're no princess."

"I don't claim to be. I've always taken whatever steps are necessary to get what I want and to protect the people I love. I'm a survivor. Are you?" She tucked her fingers into the belt at his waist and inched closer to him, close enough for the heat of her body to seep into his. "Do you want me to take the necessary step of killing Miss Lockhart? Or do you plan to wait for her to destroy us?"

"I'll take care of Hope myself."

"You'll have to get rid of the boyfriend, too, because I think dead is the only way he'll let anyone get past him now." Her fingers moved behind his zipper. Despite every urge to deny her affect on him, his body leaped in response to her touch. "Think about it, darling. Have you ever killed a man?"

"I've never killed a woman, either. That's all on you."

"You just destroy lives and let them live with the physical and mental pain you inflict. Isn't my way kinder?"

He fisted his hands at his sides, refusing to give in to her seduction. "There's not a kind bone in your body. I never asked you to clean up what I do. I never made a mistake before you got into my head and turned me into some kind of misogynistic lunatic. I never asked you to take care of me. You're a selfish, ambitious bitch like every other woman I've known."

She pressed her body against his and smiled. "And yet you stay with me. You keep coming back to me because you know I'm the only one who understands you—who can handle what you need to do."

"Stop it!" He picked her up by the shoulders and threw her onto the bed. "I don't need *handling!*" When she dared to sit up and reach for him, he flipped her onto her stomach and pushed her face into the pillow. "You make me sound like a child who needs to be taken care of. I assure you, I am no child."

She rubbed her bottom against his traitorous response to her cunning wiles, and he jerked back, giving her a few precious moments to raise her head up and catch her breath. "I protect you because I love you. I do it because you won't take care of yourself. There's nothing I won't do for you, darling."

Then she made the mistake of looking at him. He

never liked to see a woman look him straight in the eye—as though she was his equal, as though she had the right to challenge him.

He grabbed her by the hair and pushed her face back into the pillow. "Then stay away from Hope. *I* want to be the one who punishes her for betraying me. Say you understand. That you'll do nothing more to interfere. Say it!"

Her muffled voice struggled to answer. "Yes. I understand. You want to take care of Hope."

"No. I *need* to be the one who does it. Your part in this is finished. She's mine. Understood?"

He pushed harder until the only answer she could give was a nod.

He left her gasping for air on the bed as he strode from the room. The hunger was eating through his blood now. The rage consumed him. And there was only one way to curb the sickness and assuage his need. The rational part of his brain knew he'd just been manipulated into this. And yet that only fueled the compulsion to prove he was the one in control of his life.

Hope Lockhart wasn't the submissive speck on the wall he'd thought her to be. She had knowledge of things that could ruin him. And that gave her a power over him that no woman had a right to.

He grabbed his keys and slammed the door on the way out. The gasps from the woman on the bed had turned to laughter. But he refused to hear her.

It was time to prepare for the hunt.

Hope stirred restlessly as she dozed, unable to fall into the deep sleep she needed.

There were still parts of her body that were a little tender after smacking her head against the window and being jostled in her seat as her car had banged across the ditch and bounced up the hill. But she'd found a comfortable position in her own snug bed, was plenty warm beneath the sheet and quilt and even had on her old, comfy favorite—a white cotton nightgown.

But sleep eluded her because she couldn't shut down the images in her head. A white van filling up the space in her rearview mirror. Shadowed eyes above a stark white surgical mask. Golden lights bouncing off her bedroom walls. And that crawling sense of someone watching, someone she couldn't see, someone tracking her down and closing in just as surely as two red heeler mixes running down a frightened girl on a dirt-packed road, knocking her to the ground, tearing at her skin.

Hope gasped as her childhood memory blended with the grown-up nightmare of this past week. She rolled onto her back, forcing her eyes open and letting them adjust to the dim illumination from the streetlamp outside her window.

Her gaze settled on the tall silhouette of the man leaning against the doorjamb to her bedroom. Instead of being startled, she smiled. "It's not polite to stare."

Pike's low-pitched chuckle reached across the room like words of comfort. He unfolded his arms and straightened, taking a step closer to the glow from the curtains. He was still a blur until she picked up her glasses from the bedside table and put them on. His blue eyes were warm as he came into focus, but she could see the marks of fatigue lining his face. "I don't want to let you out of my sight again. Ever. This guy is more ruthless and resourceful than I imagined. I thought you'd be safe away from this neighborhood. He must have followed you out of the city."

Despite the disturbing topic and the distance of the

room between them, their voices sounded hushed, intimate somehow, in the dusky light. Maybe it was the connection to another human being who truly understood what she was going through that made this perfunctory conversation feel so soothing. "Or he knows my schedule. He knew where I'd be."

"That means he's someone you know." His shoulders lifted in a weary sigh. "Doesn't make me feel any better."

She wasn't the only one whose life had been turned upside down this week. "You need sleep, Pike."

"I've got one job, Hope. Keeping you safe. I blew it."

"I don't blame you." She pulled the covers to her chest and sat up in bed. "From the beginning, I understood the roles we had to play. You're the neighborhood cop. I'm the wedding planner. You moved in to protect me while I'm here, but if you follow me all over the city, then this guy will never make his move and you'll never catch him. Right?" He shifted on his feet, remaining silent. "And you did save me. You told me how to slow down my car. Your voice kept me from panicking. I could be dead instead of a little dinged up around the edges."

"I can see the bruises on your forehead and shoulder from here. Sorry, honey. You can't talk me out of feeling guilty." He came to the side of her four-poster bed, bringing the worn comfort of his flannel shirt and jeans into view. She could also now see the gun and badge strapped to his belt—and the concern he wore like the uniform and body armor she usually saw him in. He plucked the covers from her hands and shook the wrinkles from them. "Lie back down. I'll wait a little longer, until you fall asleep."

"But I can't sleep. My brain won't shut down. And you can't stand there forever."

"Watch me." The man took his job seriously enough that she had no doubt he'd stay at his post for days if he had to, no matter what it might cost his health or peace of mind.

But she didn't need the bodyguard keeping watch over her to chase the rapists and killers and from her dreams tonight. She needed something more than the gun and the badge. "Pike, would you stay and talk to me?"

A grin creased his scruffy jaw. "What have we been doing?"

She pulled the covers from his hands and patted the quilt beside her.

"Oh." The edge of the bed dipped when he sat and took her hand. "Better?"

Instead of being grateful for the interlocking fingers she'd grown to love, Hope pushed up onto her knees and threw her arms around his neck. "Now I am."

For one self-conscious moment, she thought she might have misread his caring nature, or that she'd pushed the limits of their charade too far. But with a breathy groan against her ear, he wound his arms around her and drew her up against his chest, lifting her off her knees and cinching her up so tight against his warmth that she felt the imprint of every button and belt buckle through the thin cotton of her nightgown. He rubbed his sandpapery jaw against her cheek and neck, catching loose tendrils of hair between them, kindling tiny sparks of friction that danced across her softer skin.

In the next moment, Hope was back on her bottom in the bed and Pike was leaving her. She quickly reached for his hand, instantly missing his strength and heat. "Pike—?"

"Shh." He squeezed her hand, whispering as he smoothed her hair away from the knot at her temple. She reached up too late to stop him from pulling her glasses off her face and setting them back on the nightstand. "I guess neither one of us is sleeping unless we do it together, right?"

Together? Wasn't that what she'd been subconsciously asking for? She held her breath when he stooped down to untie his boots. After he stripped off shoes and socks, the belt followed. She started breathing again, quickly, but soon realized her anxiety came from anticipation, maybe even a hint of impatient curiosity, not nerves or fear. Not of Pike. No, this man would always take care of her, she realized, as he carefully set his heavy black gun and badge on the bedside table. He might teach her things the same way he trained his dog, and speak plainly without a sugarcoating for anything, but his heart was pure gold. The shirt buttons came next, and Hope squinted in helpless fascination while he peeled off the blue plaid flannel and hung it on one of the bedposts. So much bare skin. So much man.

Although the jeans stayed on, he unsnapped the waist before sitting down beside her and sliding his long legs beneath the sheet. The mattress shifted and Hope tumbled into that wide expanse of naked chest. But the shock of warmth and hardness and Pike's unique musky scent quickly gave way to curiosity and then need. When Pike gathered her in his arms and lay back, Hope tentatively turned her cheek into the pillow of his shoulder. Her hand hovered above the terrain of his chest, feeling the warmth from his skin. But she was unsure exactly where to put it until he caught it and pressed it against the sleek arc of muscle over his heart.

"Breathe, Hope." His voice was husky and deep in the twilight above her. "If you don't relax, I'm going to think I'm scaring you, and neither one of us will get any sleep."

Her breath rushed out on a noisy sigh and her body closed the last bit of distance between them. Hope idly wondered if Pike could feel her breasts pillowed against his side through the thin layer of cotton knit that separated them the way she could. She'd never been draped against a man before. She liked that he was a furnace and that she seemed to be softer in places where he was harder so that their bodies could snuggle so closely together.

He must be just as aware of her body, too, because he seemed to know when she finally grew comfortable with the physical intimacy. "That's better. So what do you want to talk about?"

Her toes played nervously with the soft denim that hugged his calf. "Anything. I can't shake the feeling that he's out there, watching me. All the time. He knows everything about me and I…I don't know who he is."

His fingertips stroked up and down her arm. "No one's going to get to you tonight. My brother Alex is on one of the KCPD SWAT teams. He's perched on the roof of your friend Robin's flower shop, keeping an eye on things so we can get some sleep tonight."

"Is Hans here?" she asked.

"On the rug in your living room."

"And your brother's across the street?"

"Yes."

Hope braced her hand against Pike's chest and

pushed herself up. "So we're well protected. Why aren't you sleeping?"

"I thought you wanted to talk."

She remembered how warm her hand had been, clasped inside his in that chilly hospital room. "You were at the hospital all last night, weren't you? You need your rest."

His eyes hooded as he dropped his gaze to her chest and traced his fingertip across her collarbone. "How'd you get these?" The scars. With the slack neckline of her sleeveless gown, a man didn't need twenty/twenty vision to see them when they were this close, even in the semidarkness. "I knew you had them on your wrist, but when you were wearing that hospital gown, I saw... Some of these are skin grafts, aren't they?"

If she hadn't been snugged in the cocooning heat of the bed and his body, Hope might have frozen up. If his arm hadn't locked her against his side, she might have rolled away. If those handsome blue eyes weren't shadowed with pain, she might have closed her mouth and retreated to that quiet, lonely place inside where she normally hid from the world.

But she did none of those things. She could feel the sudden tension in him, saw the self-deprecating grin that never reached his eyes. "Asked the wrong question, didn't I?"

"It's okay." She cupped the side of his face and pressed a kiss to the corner of that false smile. He deserved to know why she was such a screwed-up woman, why he'd had to fight so hard to get her comfortable around Hans, why she had so little experience with trusting relationships. If Pike Taylor would put his life on the line for her, then the very least she could do was tell him the truth.

But it wouldn't be easy. She settled back down against him, clutching her arms between them. "My mother died in childbirth with Harry," she began. "I wasn't even two yet. I suppose Hank tried to keep us together as a family for a while. But he was never the same man after losing Mom. He blamed Harry, and I was a nonentity taking up space in the house. He started to drink and…never seemed to stop after that."

Pike groaned in lieu of a curse or condolence, and turned onto his side, throwing one of his legs over hers and drawing her more snugly into the hug of his body.

She breathed in his clean, musky smell that was simple, unadorned man, finding strength in his patience. "I became useful when I got old enough to take care of Harry and the house."

"How old were you?" His lips brushed against the crown of her hair.

"Six? Seven?" She relaxed her clenched fists and let her hands settle against the planes of his chest. "Hank drank a lot of the grocery money. He drank the mortgage payments until we were booted out of our home and went to live out in a cabin he had on one of the lakes near Branson. I kept it clean, fixed meals when I could—I was a stellar microwaver and sandwich maker."

Instead of laughing, Pike grunted a curse. "Didn't you have any family to help? Where were the social workers? My grandmother was sick with cancer for a long time, but I never doubted that she was doing her best to take care of me. Until she just couldn't any longer. I went into foster care when she went into hospice."

"She must have loved you very much."

"It was mutual. I lucked out twice in the family department with Grandma Pike and the Taylors." He went quiet for a few minutes, and Hope sneaked her right arm around his waist, holding on while he worked through his remembered grief. But then his fingers were sifting through her hair again, urging her to continue. "Did someone help you?"

Hope nodded. "My second-grade teacher reported us to DFS when I ran out of clothes that fit me. Things got better for a while. Harry and I got regular meals at school. Hank kept a part-time job with a rock-and-gravel company."

"What about the scars? Did Hank…?"

She felt the tension vibrating through every clenched muscle of Pike's body.

"Did he hurt you?"

"Not directly."

"What the hell does that mean?" The massage on her scalp stilled and Pike pulled back far enough to tilt his head down to meet her gaze. "Hope?"

She shook her head and burrowed back beneath his chin. She couldn't share the rest of it, looking into those suspicious, caring eyes. His arms stayed around her until the doubting moment passed and Hope knew she would never, ever find another man who could make her feel the trust and, yes, the hope and love that this man's blunt honesty and endless patience had nurtured in her heart.

With that stark admission of the feelings blooming inside her distracting her from the nightmarish pain this story usually invoked, Hope dug her fingertips into the reassuring warmth of his chest and finished it. "The summer I turned ten, Hank got fired for drinking on the job. Whoever his latest girlfriend was dumped him and he went on bender after bender. He'd leave the house for days sometimes. But…we had these two dogs he called the babysitters. Jack and Jilly. Doberman/heeler mixes. I suppose they were pets once, but he didn't take any better care of them than he did us."

"That son of a bitch." Pike's arms jerked around her and she laid a placating hand against the restless thump of his heart. "Babysitters?"

"Hank didn't want to lose his welfare benefits, or get in trouble with the police, so he didn't want anyone wandering onto the property or us leaving the cabin to let someone know how bad things were." For the first time tonight, tears stung her eyes, and her throat felt gritty. "Harry was so hungry that day. He was crying, and there was nothing in the house." The tears spilled over onto Pike's chest. His muscles flinched with every drop, but he said nothing. "I'd hidden a few dollars from Hank—from cleaning the neighbor's cabin—and I thought it might be enough for some milk and bread, maybe a jar of peanut butter if I could get to the store."

"But you had to get past the dogs?"

She nodded. His breathing quickened to match her own. "I fished an old, rotten meat bone out of the trash and tossed it into the yard. The dogs were starving, too. I thought I could sneak past."

"Ah, hell. Ah, hell, baby." He knew what was coming as surely as Hope.

"The dogs were doing their job. They were hungry. I smelled like garbage from the trash. And Hank came home."

"Get her!"

Footsteps pounding on the hard-packed dirt.

Tearing flesh.

"Harry was nine years old. He got Hank's gun and shot Jilly. A nine-year-old had to defend me. And I..." She couldn't breathe. She couldn't think beyond curling into a ball to protect her neck, beyond grabbing a rock and swinging it at Jack's head. "The neighbor lady heard the shot and I—"

Suddenly Hope was pulled from the nightmare by the demanding pressure of Pike's mouth against hers. "I knew you were a fighter." His body pressed her into the bed and he threaded his fingers into her hair as he kissed away the evidence of her tears. "If I had known what all you've been through, I'd never agree to this charade to draw out the Rose Red Rapist. It's too much, honey. It's too much."

Hope's hands went to his chest, instinctively bracing against his heavier weight. Then his mouth opened over hers and her fingers latched onto skin and muscle as her tongue darted out to meet his.

Fear turned to excitement. Despair turned to anticipation. Pike Taylor's fierce brand of caring chased away the nightmare and drew her back to the here and now.

Hope arched her neck as his lips skidded along the pulse at her throat, cooling the path abraded by his beard. "I'd have done it anyway," she gasped, startled by the heat pooling inside her with each rough caress. "When Detective Montgomery said I had the power to help put away that madman, I'd have volunteered, anyway."

"I know." His lips grazed her collarbone, finding nerve endings among the scarring there. Or maybe there was something in her brain that was responding to the needy tug at the strap of her nightgown, pulling it away from her shoulder so the trail of his beard and lips and tongue could continue there. The tips of her breasts beaded and rubbed against his chest, making them ache for a stronger, more insistent touch. Something sweet and hot coiled at the juncture of her thighs as his words and kisses and body caressed her skin. "You're kind of stubborn that way. You're the toughest fighter I know." He lifted his head and looked her in the eye. Even without her glasses, he was close enough to see the dilation of his pupils against the cobalt and sky-azure of his eyes. "If anyone can survive this mess, it's you."

Stubborn. Tough. A survivor.

It was as beautiful a compliment as Hope had ever received.

"Pike?" She pulled her hair off her feverish face and tucked it behind her ear. "Would you...? Can we...?"

"One of us had to ask." With a laugh, he reclaimed her mouth and rolled her onto the bed beside him.

For several minutes, there were no more words. He worked at the buttons of her gown, pressing a kiss deeper and deeper between her breasts until he groaned. Unsure whether that was frustration or arousal, she opened her mouth to ask. He held up one finger, warning her not to speak, then reached down to grab the hem of the gown and push the whole thing off over her head.

The gown flew away into the blurry darkness. The swift need of his actions startled her, excited her. But she had little time to savor each discovery of the tension building between them and inside her.

"If these aren't the prettiest things I've ever seen." Pike's hands and mouth were quickly on her breasts, squeezing, tasting, exploring the tender skin the material had hidden from him. She cried out with delight when his hot mouth closed over one aching peak and pulled it gently between his teeth. "Damn pretty."

Hope tried to keep up with every brush of his lips, every tease of his fingertips, every demand of his body. She skimmed her palms down his flanks, swirled her tongue around his taut male nipple, teasing it with her teeth the way he had her. When he bucked in response, she kissed the delicate spot and moved across his chest to see if the other was just as responsive.

Hope felt more and more feminine, more and more powerful with each sharp intake of breath, every quiver of responsive skin beneath her hands. Soon she became aware of his sturdy thigh pushing between hers. She moaned when he rubbed against her. The pressure inside her womb was sudden and intense, as if every blood cell in her body was racing to the spot to see what these new, overwhelming sensations were all about.

She was equally aware of the bulge in Pike's jeans, pressing against her hip. She was squeezing her thighs around his leg, instinctively seeking some kind of release, when he propped himself up on his elbows above her. Pike was breathing as hard as she was, so their chests kept meeting, retreating, touching again and robbing her of sense each time. His voice was husky and raw and as potently sexy as the rest of him. "Have you ever had a man in your bed, Miss Lockhart?"

Slowly, feeling the blush creep into her cheeks, she shook her head.

Pike leaned down to kiss her hard and quick as he pulled his wallet from his back pocket. "Well, get used to it. 'Cause I'm not leaving."

Taking her cue from the hands stripping her panties down her legs, Hope unzipped Pike's jeans and helped him shuck them and his boxer-briefs before they, too, sailed away into the night. Accidental, purposeful, gentle, urgent touches and whispered words filled the next few moments until Hope lay beneath him. His fingers stroked her hair, his eyes reassured, as he gave her the time she needed to get used to the feel of his hips cradled against hers, his thick, hot shaft pulsing against that most sensitive part of her.

"I'll try to be gentle," he promised. "But if anything hurts, if anything scares you, you tell me."

Hope looked up with all the love filling her heart. This was right. *He* was right. She slipped her arms around him and boldly reached down to palm his butt. "It's time to stop talking, Pike."

And then he was spreading her knees apart, nudging at her entrance, sliding inside, slowly, deeply, perfectly.

Hope gasped at how tightly he fit, how completely he filled her up, how close she could feel to one special person. Once the initial pain eased and she stroked the line of his jaw, he started moving inside her. Hope's breathing quickened. Pike's mouth was on her lips, her neck, her breasts. She gripped his back and found a rhythm that matched his. The pressure between her thighs grew almost unbearable. She wanted…she needed… "Pike?"

"That's it, honey. Let it happen."

He reached down to press the sensitive nub where they were joined and she cried out with the force of her release. While she crested the hill and marveled at the waves of tiny aftershocks pulsing inside her, Pike moved. Trusting her instincts, wanting him to know the same rapture she felt, she hooked her heels behind his thighs and opened herself to the driving force of his need. Seconds later, his arms tightened around her and he groaned against her neck. With one last thrust he tumbled over the edge inside her.

Pike collapsed on top of her and, for a moment, Hope hugged him tight around the neck, sensing that his weight and scent and the slick heat between them were the only things that could ease the sharp sensations still firing inside her. But then Pike pushed himself up, gave her a quick kiss and plopped down onto the bed beside her. He was struggling to even out his breathing, too, as he reached for her hand. "Thank you, Hope. Thank you for letting me be your first."

A few minutes later, after Pike had excused himself to the bathroom to dispose of the condom and come back with a washcloth to clean them both, Hope was still lying in the same spot on the bed. Her thoughts were floaty and the air in the room was cooling her skin. "I'm completely spent. And so relaxed. Is that normal?"

Pike laughed in the darkness and climbed back into the bed. He gathered her into his arms and pulled the cover up over them both. "That just means we did it right."

Feeling content, weary, alive and safer than she'd ever been, Hope turned her cheek into Pike's shoulder and let her eyes drift shut. There was no pretend about her feelings for Pike. This was a man she could trust. This was a man she could love.

And she did.

But the feelings were too new, too unfamiliar for her to put into words. She could barely make sense in her own head how she could, in the span of a week, lower the emotional barriers that had guarded her through so much of her life. For now, she would simply be grateful that he was kind and she was safe.

With her hand resting against the steady beat of Pike's heart, Hope fell into a deep, dreamless slumber.

SEVERAL HOURS LATER, revived by the most solid sleep he'd had in a week, Pike awoke to the brightness of the streetlamp outside the frilly curtains at the window. He slipped on his jeans for a quick check around the apartment, verifying that everything was locked and secure. He went to the front window and saluted the thumbs-up from his brother Alex on the roof across the street. He exchanged some words and licks from Hans before letting the dog settle back onto his favorite rug and returned to Hope's bedroom.

He stood in the doorway, inhaling deeply as he watched her sleep. Her hair fanned like a glorious silky mane across her pillow and the exposed curve of one beautiful breast. The cool air in the room smelled of vanilla and sex, stirring something possessive and provocative inside him.

He'd had no idea when he was stuck with this assignment a week ago that things would get personal, complicated. He wasn't a complicated kind of guy. He'd had sex before, but not like this. He'd tried relationships before, but never with anyone with so many layers and secrets and hang-ups and curiosity and courage as Hope. He'd dated prettier women, more experienced women, women who actually talked to him the first time they'd met.

But he couldn't remember any woman getting under his skin and getting inside his head the way Hope Lockhart did.

"So what are you going to do about it, Taylor?" he whispered into the shadows.

This was supposed to be a job. He had a mission to complete. The safety of his beat, maybe of the entire city, rested on his shoulders. If he was smart, he'd grab his gun and badge, take a cold shower, brew a pot of coffee and sit up with the dog in the living room, keeping watch.

Instead, he unsnapped his jeans and dropped them

on the floor before crawling under the covers with Hope again.

She stirred when he brushed that decadent fall of hair away from her porcelain skin. Those big lake-gray eyes opened like shadowy pools in the darkness and she reached for him. "Hey. I was thinking…"

"Uh-oh." He shouldn't get this kind of rush watching a blush stain her cheeks and creep down her neck. He shouldn't be this curious to see just how far down that blush could go. "What is it?"

"I know that some people do it more than once. Could we? I may never get this chance again."

The tips of those lush breasts were already teasing pebbles against his chest, waking his body. "I doubt that, honey."

"Please?" She was doing that ticklish thing with her toes again. "If you have another condom, that is. If you want."

Yeah. He wanted.

It was swifter, needier, this time as he pulled Hope on top of him and taught her a couple of new things about making love. He made it as good as he knew how, driving her to the edge of her release as she took him right to the brink with her.

And when he drove himself home inside her, pouring out the essence of everything in him, Pike knew something had changed. Terribly. Irrevocably.

This woman wasn't just his to protect.

She was his.

Chapter Eleven

Pike felt a sudden chill when Hope rolled away, taking her sweet warmth and half the covers with her.

"Is that your phone or mine?" she asked.

His.

Hope turned on the lamp beside her and tried to find her glasses and cell while he pulled his jeans down from the bedpost. He didn't need glasses, the lamp or the dusky, predawn twilight to see his phone screen flashing like an alert, or to have a bad feeling about why anyone would call at this hour.

He pushed the talk button and tucked the phone between his ear and shoulder, slipping into his shorts and jeans as soon as he read Alex's name on the screen. "What is it?"

He had a very bad feeling before his brother even spoke.

"Just spotted a white van with a silver bumper half a mile north of your position," Alex reported. "It's headed this way. Do you want me to intercept it?"

This was it. He was here. The Rose Red Rapist was coming for Hope.

And Pike was damn well going to put a stop to that man's reign of terror over the city. And her.

"Negative," Pike answered, grabbing his shirt. "Call Montgomery and give him a sit-rep."

"You need me to call in backup? SWAT Two is on duty. The team could be here in ten minutes."

"Pike?"

He threaded his holster onto the belt of his jeans and hurried to the window, barely hearing the soft whisper from across the bed. Alex's SWAT training and gear gave him a tactical advantage Pike couldn't match. But he parted the curtains and peeked through the blinds anyway, hoping to glimpse a target where he could focus the red alert pumping through his blood.

But beyond a few parked cars, traffic was almost nonexistent. Their unsub would see the cops coming and disappear back to one of the nearby thoroughfares or the interstate. "Negative. Too big a presence will scare this guy away. Besides, this is our bust. We've been working too damn long and hard on this case. We'll take him down."

"Understood, little bro." Despite the nickname, Alex was all special weapons and tactics right now. "I'll maintain my position and give you an update if he changes course. Good luck, Pike."

"Thanks for having my back, Alex."

"Roger that. Taylor out."

Pike tucked the phone into the front pocket of his jeans and dropped to the bed to put on his socks and boots. Half a mile away? Maybe two or three stoplights to catch him between here and there? If he was lucky. Pike had a matter of minutes—seconds, maybe—to gear up and get into position to catch this guy. He quickly tied the second boot and stood.

"Is it him?" Hope had pulled the quilt with her off the bed and wrapped herself in it to bar his path out the bedroom door. He'd already seen the lush beauty of her full figure, and had caressed every one of her scars, so he doubted it was modesty that made her cover up. She was afraid. Shutting down. Hiding herself from the world that had done her such harm again.

He needed to say something. He needed to tell her that she meant something to him and that last night was hot and that maybe, one day, when life was sane and safe for them again, they could…what? What was he going to do? What did he want to do about Hope?

"I gotta go." Seriously? That was the best he could come up with?

That knot of consternation dented the skin above her glasses. "Okay."

Frustrated by his inability to say the right thing at the right time, and feeling the clock ticking down as the van approached, Pike snaked his hand behind her neck and pulled her up onto her toes, planting a hard kiss on her soft mouth before setting her aside and darting into the hallway.

"You're a fighter," he called out over his shoulder. "Remember that. Hans! *Hier!*"

He grabbed his keys, his flak vest and the leash as the big dog bounded to his side. Pike suited up, before putting the harness and badge on Hans. Hope had followed him out, still clutching the quilt to her breasts and bottom, still looking at him with the fear and questions in her eyes.

Say something.

The phone vibrated against his thigh. His brother was calling again. The mark must be close now. "I need you to lock the doors behind me. Stay put. I'll be back."

Then he and Hans were out the door and running

down the stairs. He opened his truck and put the dog inside as he took Alex's call. "What's up?"

"The van's stopped at the light at the top of the street. He'll go past you in about thirty seconds." Pike started the engine and pulled the truck up to the edge of the parking lot entrance, leaving his lights off to stay hidden until the last possible moment. "I'm ready."

"Montgomery was at HQ. He's on his way. Fensom's already en route." The tenor of Alex's voice changed to that of a soldier, ready for battle. "Light's changing. I'm on my way down to back you up."

Pike felt the same cagey readiness running through his veins. "Roger that. Taylor out."

Phone in pocket. Breathe deeply. Grip wheel.

"And here...we..."

Go!

As expected, the boxy white van slowed in front of Hope's shop. But the driver must have spotted Pike's truck, even in the shadows. With a squeal of rubber clawing to find traction on the pavement, the van driver pushed his lights up to bright, momentarily blinding Pike, and floored it.

Since he'd been made, Pike flipped on his own lights and the siren and pulled out onto the street as the van sped past. The truck bounced over the curb and picked up speed to gain ground on the van. With the T-intersection at the south end of the block, the unsub was going to have to either slow down or fly around a corner and risk rolling the van. Either way, Pike intended to stop him.

Thankfully, there was little traffic, but the driver was already pushing his luck, fishtailing into the side of one parked car as he veered into the opposite lane to try to make a wider turn. Pike pushed the accelerator closer to the floor and held on tighter. The guy whipped back into his lane and bounced off another car, shooting up sparks as metal scraped against metal.

Pike saw a couple turning the corner on the sidewalk up ahead. Their looks of panic were unmistakable as they jumped back toward the shelter of the nearest building. Another car screeched to a stop and shifted into Reverse, backing out of the intersection as the two vehicles raced toward it.

"Slow down!"

Pike's engine roared with power. His siren screamed in his ears, but he could still make out other sirens in the distance. Too far in the distance. And Alex was at least half a block behind him.

"We've got to stop him, Hansie." The dog was panting in rhythm with the charged adrenaline pumping Pike's heart. "It's you and me."

He quickly glanced ahead. Nobody knew this part of town the way he did. He knew every citizen, every corner, every curb. Coffee shop on the left. Dance bar on the right. Yarn shop straight ahead. They were all closed for the night, but owners lived in the apartments above them. Security guards sat in offices and patrolled their buildings. A couple of homeless guys liked the alley off to the east when the night wasn't too cold. If traffic was clear, that left the abandoned warehouse around the corner to the west that hadn't been reclaimed yet.

Target acquired.

He called in the location, updating the chase to Dispatch, alerting traffic cops to clear the streets, telling his task force teammates where they could finally get their man. He reported his intent and hung up the radio.

Pressing the accelerator down to the floor, Pike

raced up behind the van, targeting the left side of that shiny steel bumper. Closer. Closer.

The van's brake lights flashed. "Gotcha."

Pike rammed the truck's front end into the rusting taillight of the van and sent it skidding around the corner. With a big white target and a clear sidewalk in front of him, Pike T-boned the van. It jumped the curb and Pike hit his brakes, letting the truck's momentum shove the van straight into the crumbling brick facade of the abandoned building.

His seat belt caught and held as the truck's front end crumpled and the windshield cracked. Hans woofed in protest at the wild ride and abrupt stop.

But they were both okay, and the damn van wasn't going anywhere. One rear wheel was shredded and one in the front wasn't even touching the ground.

"Hans, *bleib!*" Pike reassured the dog of the need to stay put, unhooked his seat belt and climbed out of the steaming truck.

He drew his Glock as he ran to the front of the van. "KCPD! Take your hands off the wheel!" He opened the folding door and charged up the steps, his gun pointed straight at the driver's head. "Payback's a bitch, isn't it? You run my girl off the road—I run you…"

The adrenaline short-circuited into confusion. Gray hair. Prison tats. This wasn't right.

"Officer Taylor." Hank Lockhart massaged his shoulder and ran his tongue along the lip he'd split open, having smacked one or both on the bloodied side window.

Pike glanced into the back of the van. Empty. Spotlessly clean. And there were no other seats inside. This didn't make sense. Where…?

The gray eyes might be bleary with pain or booze, but the old coot was laughing.

The amused, malevolent sound galvanized Pike and he leveled his gun at the ruddy target of the bastard's nose. Questions could be answered later. "Hands up, Lockhart."

There were lights flashing in the corner of his vision now. Help had arrived. Not that he'd need it to take this lousy excuse for a man down. As soon as Lockhart's hands settled on top of his head, Pike holstered his weapon and pulled out his handcuffs. He slapped one end around Lockhart's wrists and reached for the other hand.

"Ow, man." Lockhart swore as Pike jerked his injured arm behind him and locked the other cuff around his wrist. "I really took a shot to my shoulder."

"And your daughter took on a pair of starving dogs because of you. I don't hear her complaining." Cars were stopping, and guns and detectives were charging forward as Pike dragged him out and shoved his face into the side of the van. Pike kicked the old man's legs apart and searched him, pulling out a pocketknife, a wallet and a thick long envelope. He ripped it open and found a stack of hundred-dollar bills inside. "Where'd you get this?"

The old man turned his head with a smug grin. "I'm gettin' my money out of that girl one way or the other."

Pike braced his forearm behind Lockhart's neck and shoved him back against the van. "What are you talking about?"

"Taylor!" Spencer Montgomery holstered his weapon as he jogged up. With a nod, his partner, Nick Fensom, jumped inside the van to give it the same once-over

Pike had done. He took the cash and knife Pike handed him. "Is this our guy?"

Pike stepped back, shaking his head as the senior detective spun the culprit to face him. "This is Hank… Henry Lockhart Sr."

"Hope's father?"

Nick jumped down from the van's steps and holstered his weapon. "My grandmother doesn't keep her bathroom as spotless as that van. The whole thing reeks of disinfectant." He pulled out his cell phone. "I'll call Annie to bring her kit. Whatever was back there has been cleaned within an inch of its life." He nodded to the gray-haired man in handcuffs. "Who's this douche?"

"Our eyewitness's father." Montgomery pulled his cell phone from his suit jacket and pulled up a picture. "The van matches Hope's description. But he's not our guy. She'd have recognized her own father, wouldn't she? Even with a mask?"

Pike glanced behind him, taking in the skid marks and wreckage, unmarked vehicles and black-and-whites with flashing lights blocking off the three-way intersection. This was one hell of a show for downtown Kansas City at five in the morning.

One hell of a distraction.

Suspicion lit a fuse inside him. "Run his priors," he advised the senior detective. He walked out past the back of his truck, gazing as far up the street as the streetlamps and strobe effect of the flashing lights would let him. What was out of place? What was missing? "Lockhart did time in Jeff City. I'm sure he was incarcerated for at least some of the Rose Red Rapist assaults."

His brother Alex walked up with Nelda Sapphire in handcuffs. "This one was following you in a compact heap of junk. Didn't think much of it until you did your fancy driving. Once you crashed, she pulled off in an alley and started running the other direction."

"Not a word, Nelda," Hank warned.

"Shut up." Pike and Detective Montgomery both had the same idea.

"Probably his getaway," Pike guessed, rejoining the others. If this was their unsub's van, the one Hope had identified, there were only a couple of reasons why Hank would be driving it. And the coincidence that he'd stolen this particular van wasn't very likely. "Drive the van someplace and drop it off, then she picks him up."

"This isn't your guy?" Alex asked.

No. But he could lead them to him.

"Tell me about the money, Hank." Pike resisted the urge to drive his fist into that split lip and opted for a threat Hope's opportunistic father might answer to. "We've already got you on speeding, reckless driving, assault, attempted assault—"

"What? I never."

"—and accessory to rape and murder. How much time do you want to spend with your old friends in lockup?"

"Tell him, Hank," Nelda urged. Mascara ran down her face as she cried. "Or I will."

Surrounded by two armed detectives, a cop in full SWAT gear and an angry Pike who used every inch of his six feet four inches of height to back the coward against the van, Hank finally muttered something useful. "Some guy paid me five thousand to drive his van past Hope's shop."

"Some guy? What guy?"

"I don't know." The guy looked smaller and meaner, backed into a corner like this. But he knew he had no place to go. "He found Nelda and me sleeping in her car last night. Black pants and a jacket was all I could see in the side mirror. Came at us from behind and knocked on the window. Said he saw me hanging around Hope's shop a couple of times. Told me not to turn around and look at his face, and for that kind of money, I didn't."

Decoy.

"Hope." Pike ran to his truck.

That's what was off. There'd been no cars parked in front of Hope's shop when the van drove past. And he'd just spotted a light-colored SUV there.

Even the unflappable Spencer Montgomery revealed a spike of temper. "You set up your own daughter?"

"She wouldn't help me, so I helped myself."

Montgomery grabbed Hank Lockhart and handed him off to a pair of approaching uniforms. "Get this trash out of here."

Pike's truck was toast. The shop wasn't that far. He opened the back door and grabbed Hans's leash.

"Taylor!" Detective Montgomery caught the door and closed it after Hans jumped out.

"Pike?" Alex fell into step beside them as they jogged across the intersection. "Talk to me, bro."

"Get everyone back to Fairy Tale Bridal. He's going after Hope."

Then there was only Pike and his partner and a long city block to run. "Go, boy!"

HOPE DIDN'T WASTE any time after Pike and Hans left. She pulled on underwear, jeans and a sweater, and grabbed her phone and keys before unbolting the door and running barefoot down the stairs.

Whatever was going on was something bad. And even though she had questions about last night with

Pike, and even more questions about tomorrow, she knew that something big was breaking on the task force investigation. Pike needed to deal with the danger his brother had alerted him to, and he needed her to nod her head and do what he said.

She pulled open the door at the bottom of the stairs and immediately turned the dead bolt on the outside door of the vestibule, securing access to both the shop and her apartment. She peered out the door into the rose-tinted darkness of early morning and saw that Pike's truck was gone. There'd be time to ask questions later, she hoped. Time enough for Pike to come back safely. Time to wrap up this hellish mission and end their fake engagement.

Hope held on to the door handle and stretched up on tiptoe, trying to see over the fence and hedge that lined the parking lot. Were those flashing lights bouncing off the tops of the buildings? Pike's was one truck. Just how many emergency vehicles were out there? What was going on? Was someone hurt? Was Pike?

Obeying common sense as much as curiosity, she unlocked the inside door to the shop and went in to check the front door and windows there. Her bare toes made no sound on the cold tile and carpeting, and she left the lights off so no one would be alerted to movement inside the store.

She peeked through the mannequins in the window display and saw a black-and-white police car with flashing lights parked sideways across the street, down by the coffee shop. Had there been an accident?

Without stopping to ponder an answer, she continued to the front door between the displays and jiggled the handle. Locked. Good. She was safe.

Now she could spend a few seconds pressing her

cheek to the glass to see farther down the street. Where was Pike's truck? All she saw were police cars and flashing lights. She almost smiled with relief. Had they caught the Rose Red Rapist? Had the sting operation worked?

Hope breathed a sigh of relief and pulled her phone from her pocket. How needy and inappropriate would it be if she called Pike right now and asked him for answers? Asked him to come back to her? Asked him...

The scent of a powerful cologne, tainted with undertones of vinegar or disinfectant stung her nose.

Oh, God. Her pulse thundered in her ears. She wasn't alone in the shop.

Had someone snuck in before she'd gotten the outside door locked? Who else would have a key?

She slipped her thumb over the screen of her phone and pushed Pike's number and the call button. Fear kicked into panic and her fingers trembled as she tried to slide her key into the lock to get out the door. But the reflection taking shape behind her in the window warned her it was already too late.

Screaming at the familiar white mask, Hope turned to defend herself. But his arm was already swinging. He hit her in the side of the head and she was unconscious before she hit the floor.

"How long do you think it's been?" Detective Montgomery asked.

Pike didn't have time to piece together clues and figure this out intellectually, so his brother answered. "Fifteen minutes, twenty, tops, sir. Pike left the building at 5:10 a.m. I picked up Miss Sapphire at quarter after. It's not five-thirty yet."

"The street's blocked to the south, so he had to go

north. Traffic Patrol would have spotted a speeding car, so he can't have gotten far. I'm calling in every favor I've got for this manhunt." Montgomery pulled out his phone. "Nick's already going door to door. Maggie Wheeler, Dr. Kate and her friend Sheriff Harrison are on their way. I'll contact Dispatch and get every available uniform here ASAP."

"Belay that phone call, sir." Rank didn't matter when it came to Hope. Pike was giving the orders now.

They didn't need manpower. They didn't need men.

Pike knelt beside Hope's glasses and shattered phone and let Hans sniff the white nightgown he held in his gloved hand. "I need you to do this for me, boy. I need you to find her. Please."

The German shepherd whined and tilted his head to one side. Pike could tell from his excited panting that he had the scent and was ready to work. But his partner wasn't used to being asked. He was used to being led. Pike pushed to his feet and opened the shop's front door. "Hans! *Such!*"

HOPE CAME TO with a start. The pungent liquid splashing on her chest and neck acted like smelling salts, piercing the fog of her headache and waking her to the cool lights of the room above her.

Above?

Automatically, she reached up to adjust her glasses. But both hands came up, and she hissed at the sharp pinch at her wrists. They were duct-taped together.

Half-blind? Bound?

Fear sharpened her senses further and Hope squinted to bring something—anything—into focus. Colorless walls reflected a single light hanging overhead. From the angle of things, she must be lying on the floor. She couldn't make out any windows, couldn't tell if it was morning or night.

But her other senses worked just fine. The cold liquid hit her belly and she shrieked. Vinegar? She jerked away from the smelly dousing and rolled over a sheet of plastic that popped and crackled when she moved. Beneath the plastic, something padded protected her from the hardness of the brown floor. A mattress. The air was chilly and stale, with no moving air. And she was shivering because her sweater had been cut or ripped and pushed aside, leaving her in a bra and blue jeans for protection and warmth.

And then she saw the black shadow moving past her feet and remembered the reflection in the glass.

Hope startled, tried to scoot away. But a strong hand clamped over her ankle and pulled her back into place. She was going to die. She was going to be horribly violated, made to suffer and then she would die.

"Where am I? Who are you? Why are you doing this?" she asked in rapid succession. Oh, God, she was in terrible trouble. Where was Pike? Did he know how much she loved him? Would it matter? Did she have any chance of saving herself? "Do you have my glasses? I can't see," she admitted as the first hot tear ran across her cheek to her ear.

The man laughed.

Finally, he spoke. "I've been such a fool." Five simple words and she felt light-headed again. Sick to her stomach. Heartbroken. She knew that voice. All this time…so many conversations. And she'd never had any idea of his dark, dangerous secret. "You never saw me at all that night, did you? With those eyes, in the shadows, you never really could. And to think I believed the lies you told."

Hope blinked away the tears that burned her eyes. "Brian? Brian Elliott? You're…"

"Yes." Something silky soft and sweetly fragrant touched her nose and she jerked away from the sickening caress. A red rose. "I'm the devil the police can never catch. I'm the man terrorizing the women of this city. I'm teaching every greedy, selfish witch that she's not everything she thinks she is. I'm the Rose Red Rapist." He crawled over her, dropping the rose beside her as he came into view. He was wearing that glaring white surgeon's mask over the bottom half of his face. But the eyes above the mask were dark and clear, and sadly familiar. "But you're never going to tell anyone that."

He reached down and unsnapped her jeans. When the zipper began to slide apart, she shook off the shock of never knowing what an evil man her mentor and friend had been—of never even suspecting how sadistic he could be. "Stop it!"

She bucked beneath him, clawed the air to stop his hands. But she was helpless. Trapped.

Brian picked up a bottle, although she couldn't make out the contents. "Women are filthy creatures, you know. You can't trust them." He poured the liquid onto a cloth and she realized that was the vinegar mixture he'd thrown on her earlier. Hope sucked in her breath when he laid the cloth on her stomach and started to bathe her. "They take everything you have—your money, your trust, your heart—and they grind it into dust beneath their feet. They use you. They humiliate you."

She arched her back, trying to escape the cloth sliding over her skin. "I never did."

"I thought you were different, Hope. I made you into the success you are. I coaxed you out of your shell and taught you to trust your vision. I gave you a building to live and work in—"

"I bought that building." She snatched at the cloth, but he pulled it beyond her reach. "You invested in my shop."

"I never thought you would betray me. You were always so dutiful. So appreciative."

"I worked hard to get where I am. I thought you were proud of me."

"I was. And then…"

"What? What did I do, Brian? What did any of those women you hurt do to you? Bailey Austin? LaDonna Chambers?"

"You're all like Mara."

"Your ex-wife?" He freshened the washrag and slipped it beneath the elastic of her panties. "Why are you doing this?"

"You humiliated me. You played me for a fool."

"Stop it, Brian." She tried to sit up, but he shoved her back down. "You don't want to do this."

"I've never heard you talk this much before, Hope. I don't like it." He reached across her and came back with a box cutter that he trailed against her cheek.

Hope jerked her head away from the sharp blade. "The police will find you. You won't get away with this."

"I've gotten away with this for years. A mousy little slut like you isn't going to change that."

She heard the ripping sound of tape before she felt the vibration of a slamming door from somewhere beneath them. "Where are we?"

"Shut up."

"Brian—"

"Shut up!" He slapped her across the mouth, stunning her long enough for him to press a piece of duct tape over her mouth. He jerked her jeans down her hips and Hope screamed helplessly behind the tape.

Do something. Make a noise. Help them find you.

If there was ever a time in her life she needed her voice to be heard, it was right now.

While Brian unhooked his belt, Hope reached up and peeled the tape from her lips. "Help me! Help—"

When his fist came down, she raised her hands to deflect the blow. Brian grabbed her wrists and pushed them over her head, tearing skin beneath the tape as she thrashed and screamed. He lay across her, reaching for something. She kicked. She twisted. She heard the clatter of heavy objects hitting metal and wood. He grunted. She jerked. Brian sat up, his weight straddling her body and crushing the breath from her lungs. He raised his hand and she saw the hammer he'd pulled from the toolbox beside her.

Hope screamed.

"KCPD!" She heard a loud bang and the splintering of solid wood. Brian turned. "Hans! *Fass!*"

A blur of black and tan leaped at billionaire Brian Elliott and knocked him to the floor.

Hope tumbled off the mattress as Brian cursed and screamed. She'd heard ferocious snarls like that once before in her life. Even dazed and frightened, without her glasses, she knew exactly what was happening. There was the initial blow that knocked the wind and sense from a body. The bruising punctures. The tearing skin.

"Hope? Hope!" Pike pulled Hope to her feet and tucked her behind the broad wall of his back. "How bad are you hurt?"

"I'm okay," she whispered. She pulled up her jeans

and fastened them as best she could with her clothes wet and her hands still bound. She curled her fingers into Pike's belt and moved with him as he pointed his gun at Brian Elliott. "I'm okay," she repeated with more strength.

"Hans! *Platz!*" In a heartbeat, the growling stopped and the big dog sat back on his haunches and lay down.

"Damn." Brian writhed on the floor, clutching his injured arm to his stomach. "Filthy beast! You've killed me."

"Shut up, Elliott, or I'll let him do it."

"I need to wash. I need to clean it off."

Pike inched closer with the gun and pressed it against Brian's skull. "Don't move."

Other than breathing hard and moaning in pain, Brian didn't.

"Come here, baby." Pike shifted his gun to one hand and reached behind him to hug Hope to his side. "How many doors do I have to break down to get to you?" He pressed a kiss to the crown of her hair and then turned his attention to the man bleeding on the plastic-covered mattress. "Brian Elliott, you are under arrest for kidnapping and assault on Hope Lockhart. Other charges will be filed against you. You have the right to remain silent." More footsteps stamped up the stairs and blurry figures she couldn't recognize charged into the room. "You have the right to an attorney. If you can't—"

"We've got it, Taylor." Hope recognized Spencer Montgomery's voice. "Nick, cuff this bastard." The detective's red hair came into focus as Pike backed away from the man on the floor. "Are you okay, Miss Lockhart?" He looked over his shoulder and shouted, "Let's get a bus here and have this woman looked at."

She nodded and he faded away again as Pike turned

her away from the black uniforms and plainclothes officers storming into the room. "Come on, honey. You've
done your part." He pushed her several steps out of the
way while he holstered his weapon and ripped apart
the Velcro fastenings on his flak vest. "You've done a
hell of a lot more than we had the right to ask of you."

"I can't see anything, Pike. I feel so lost."

"Here. Probably should have left them at the crime
scene, but..." The first thing Hope saw when Pike
slipped her glasses onto her nose was the clear blue
gaze of his eyes. They were dark with concern, lined
with fatigue—and the most beautiful sight she could
hope to see.

Joy and relief rushed through her before caution and
common sense could, and Hope stretched up onto her
toes and looped her bound arms around Pike's neck.
"You found me. You saved me. Just like you promised."

His arms cinched around her back and he lifted
her clear off the floor, turning his face into her hair.
"Hans found you. He followed your scent across two
city streets and up three flights of stairs. He's the one
who saved you."

Hope struggled to find the floor again, to stand on
her own two feet and frame Pike's anguished face between her hands. "Who trained Hans? Who busted up
that door so he could get to me? Who never gave up on
me?" She pulled his head down and kissed him, just the
way he'd taught her how. "Thank you," she whispered
as she settled back on her feet. "Thank you."

Without a *you're welcome* or *no problem* or *my pleasure, ma'am,* Pike pushed his vest over his head and
dropped it to the floor. He picked up the very box cutter Brian had threatened her with and sliced through
the tape on her wrists. Then he pulled off her ruined

sweater and replaced it with the blue flannel shirt he wore.

And while Pike buttoned her up, the rest of the room came into focus. They were at a construction site. She recognized the two-by-fours framing open walls that had been covered in plastic.

"Secure this location," Montgomery ordered. There were several voices talking now. Clipped commands and "yes, sirs."

"This crazy guy has created his own sterile room." That was Detective Fensom. "He could move this setup from building site to building site. No wonder we could never come up with a crime scene. Annie's going to have a field day processing this one."

"So let's get everyone out of here before we contaminate any more of it." Spencer Montgomery was clearly the man in charge. "Get Chief Taylor on the line and wake up the commissioner. I'm escorting this guy downtown myself."

"I want a doctor and my lawyer," Brian protested.

"Bring Miss Lockhart, too."

"Yes, sir," Pike answered, catching a T-shirt that one of the uniformed officers tossed to him, and slipping it on over his head. "Need anything before we go downtown?" he asked her.

Another kiss? A chance to erase the guilt that lingered in his eyes? But what if he didn't want her to ask those things, anymore? They didn't have to pretend to be a couple anymore.

They were a cop and a shopkeeper.

They were friends.

"Yes, wait." She couldn't leave yet, not without the rest of her protection team. "Hans! *Hier!*"

The German shepherd jumped to his feet and trot-

ted over to her. *"Setzen!"* He sat down beside her and
Hope knew an urge to drop to her knees and hug him
around the neck, too. But training was a slow, repeti-
tive process. And she still had a ways to go to completely move past those long-ingrained fears. But she
did reached down and scratch around his soft, furry
ears. "Good boy, Hansie. Good boy."

If Pike hadn't laced his fingers with hers just then,
she might have burst into tears. Instead, she latched
onto the strength of his hand, to the strength he'd revealed inside her.

She had a feeling she'd need every last bit of that
strength to get through the rest of the day—maybe, to
get through the rest of her life.

"Thank you, Hans." She petted the dog one more
time, then headed to the door with Pike on her left and
Hans on her right. She was safe. Kansas City was safe.
It was enough. "Thank you both."

Chapter Twelve

How long were Spencer Montgomery and Nick Fensom going to keep grilling Hope?

When Pike stepped off the elevator onto the third floor at Fourth Precinct headquarters, her curly mane of toffee hair was the first thing he spotted. Without the overbearing assistance of either her attorney or her mentor, Hope was sitting across from Detective Montgomery at his desk, going over some kind of paperwork. Maybe it was just the formal approval of her statement. And maybe the detectives were demanding something more from a brave woman who had already given far too much.

They had Brian Elliott dead to rights on kidnapping and assault charges, thanks to Hope. And the task force was certain they could get him on the multiple rape charges now that he could be compelled to give a DNA sample to match the evidence they had on file at the crime lab. If they got a witness to come forward who could put Elliott at any one of those previous crimes, they'd have a slam-dunk case for the D.A.'s office, and the man would never get out of prison.

Pike leaned against the sergeant's counter, scrubbing the tight muscles of his jaw as he watched over the conversation from a distance. Even though the detectives had let her shower and put on a borrowed set of gray KCPD sweats after Annie Hermann had taken her clothes and Pike's shirt, and processed Hope for evidence, the grueling marathon of wrapping up the details of the task force investigation had to be wearing her out. Hell, Pike was exhausted. And he hadn't been struck in the head, kidnapped and nearly assaulted.

She'd sat through the task force briefing with his team, eaten a lousy cafeteria lunch and identified Elliott in a lineup, first with, and then without, that neurotic surgical mask he'd been wearing that first night he'd nearly run her off the road with his van. Pike had even had time to run down to the locker room to shower and shave and put on a clean uniform while Hope met with Commissioner Cartwright-Masterson and Pike's uncle, Precinct Chief Mitch Taylor, to receive an official departmental thank-you for a citizen going above and beyond to help serve and protect her community.

They'd have to feed her dinner soon if they kept Hope here much longer. And Pike wanted that opportunity for himself. He wanted to take her home, at least. Let her change into something demure and girly, and run around barefoot. He wanted to tuck her into bed and watch over her and teach her a thing or two more about making out and making love—or maybe he'd let her teach him since she seemed to have such a flair for making him crazy in all the right ways.

"Earth to Edison." A bump on his shoulder roused him from his thoughts. "Yo, Pike."

Pike pushed away from the sergeant's desk and looked down to see his brother Alex grinning up at him. "Now what?"

He knew that look. Alex was cooking up something

that was going to either embarrass him or put him in his place.

"I was just wondering how long you were going to stand here looking at that woman before you work up the nerve to go over there and do something about it."

"Do something about what?"

Alex punched him again. "How much you love her."

Pike shrugged off Alex's annoying attempt to get a reaction out of him. "It was a fake relationship, Alex. An undercover op."

"Uh-huh." Alex crossed his arms in front of him, mimicking Pike's stance. "I saw the look on your face when you realized Elliott had her. That wasn't worry that you'd blown the assignment—that was a man who had his heart ripped out of his chest because he thought he might lose the woman he loves."

Surprised by his brother's serious tone, Pike released a heavy breath and admitted his fear. "What if it was just a job to her? Hope doesn't have a lot of experience with men. Now that she knows she can do anything she sets her mind to, be with anyone she wants—what if she decides I'm not what she wants?"

"Seriously?" Alex shook his head. "You're a Taylor. You're KCPD. You're *my* brother. She'd be crazy not to want you."

Something warm and free from doubt blossomed inside Pike at his brother's vehement defense. He grinned his appreciation. "You're getting soft on me, Alex."

Hope and the detectives all stood and shook hands, giving every indication that at last they were done.

"Me? Soft?" Alex nudged Pike forward, quickly moving past the mushy stuff. "I'm not the one who's afraid to tell a woman that he loves her. You go up to her, maybe take some flowers, think about your favorite greeting card and what it says. Tell her she's pretty or sexy or—"

Pike palmed Alex in the face and shoved him away. "I got this."

So this was it.

Hope had stayed as long as she could at precinct headquarters, waiting for the chance to share a private conversation with Pike before they had to return to their normal, *real,* lives tomorrow. Before they went back to being the neighborhood cop and the shy shopkeeper he tipped his hat to.

Now he was closing the door to one of the meeting rooms behind him, filling up the small space with his size and earthy scent and easy confidence. She paced off the length of the conference table, wishing she had time to change into something more feminine, wishing she wasn't bruised and scarred and so embarrassingly new at this personal relationship thing.

"Pike—"

"Hope—"

They had started together.

Her cheeks heated with embarrassment. "You go ahead."

"No, you first."

Fine. She could do this. She tugged the sleeves of the sweatshirt she wore down over her fingers and curled the long cuffs inside her fists. "I just wanted…" She tipped her face up to his and smiled. No need to be nervous when what she had to say was true. "I wanted to thank you."

He leaned his hip against the table and sat on the corner. "For what?"

"Saving my life. Being patient. Teaching me not to

be so afraid of dogs." She moved a couple of steps closer and gestured toward the detectives' desks beyond the door. "Thank you for finally getting my father out of my life. And for showing me how to love. You were my first, Pike. In more ways than you'll ever know."

"Like I said, you have all the right instincts, honey. You just needed the confidence to act on them." He plucked at a nonexistent piece of lint on his black slacks. "What do your instincts say about us?"

If she could survive this past week, then she could find the courage to say three words. "I love you." His fingers stopped playing and his head jerked up. "But I want you to know that I would never hold you to any sham of a relationship. If all we can be is friends, I'm okay with that."

"I'm not."

"Excuse me?"

Pike reached for her hand and pulled her closer, adjusting his position so he could pull her between his knees and slip his fingers inside her baggy shirt to rest his hands at either side of her waist. "Look, I'm going to say this just as plain and direct as I know how. I love you, Hope Lockhart. You deserve a happily-ever-after more than any woman I know." He twirled a fingertip into a long tendril of hair that had fallen across her cheek, and tucked it back behind her ear. She leaned her cheek into his hand when it lingered there. "If you'd be interested, I'd like to hire your services to create the wedding of your dreams. I'd like you to be the bride and I want to be the groom. I'll even put on one of those damned tuxes. I want the real thing with you."

"Yes."

"Yes? This is what you really want, too? I'm a real catch. I talk to dogs, I like to fish, I don't always say what I mean." Sarcasm bled into his voice, but she refused to hear it.

Hope slipped her fingers around his crisp black collar and drifted closer to the addictive warmth of his body. "But you *do* what you mean. Let me make this just as plain and direct as I can, too. My answer is yes." The doubts around her heart vanished like magic and she leaned in to meet his kiss. "*You're* my happily-ever-after."

* * * * *

Don't miss the conclusion of USA TODAY
bestselling author Julie Miller's
THE PRECINCT: TASK FORCE when
YULETIDE PROTECTOR BRIDE
goes on sale in December 2013.
Look for it wherever
Harlequin Intrigue books are sold!

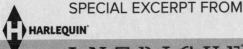
He reached for the glass of water on the nightstand and
stopped dead. The wide gold band on the ring finger of his
left hand glinted in the sunlight. He rubbed at his eyes, but
it didn't go away. He was married?

His head and stomach protested as he took in the strewn
clothing along with this new information.

No. Impossible. No way he'd forget his own wedding or
the inevitable events leading up to it. No way he'd marry a
stranger—and Ginger Olin, CIA operative, fit that description.
This had to be some ruse she'd invented to preserve her cover.

He couldn't make sense of the vague scenes flitting through
his mind. She owed him some answers. This time when he
pushed to his feet, he kept moving forward despite the sudden
tilt of the room. He was grateful when the wall kept him from
hitting the floor. He pounded a fist on the bathroom door. "Get
out here."

She opened the door and a steamy cloud of spicy vanilla scent washed over him.

"Oh, dear," she said with a sly smile as her gaze slid over his body like a touch. One long fingertip trailed across his jaw. "You're looking rough." She opened the door wider. "Come on in. A shower will fix you right up."

Was that a bit of Irish in her voice this morning? If so, was it real? He'd done a little investigating after their last meeting and knew she had a talent for accents.

She tucked herself under his arm, keeping him steady as she walked him past the long vanity. Something about the gesture felt familiar.

"Did you do this last night?"

"We can talk about last night when your head's clear." She eased back but didn't quite let go. "Steady?"

Barely. "Yes."

"Cold or hot?"

"Pardon?"

"The shower," she clarified, her eyes quickly darting down to his groin and back up again.

"Cold."

"All righty."

The secrets are only just starting.
Find out what happens next in
READY, AIM…I DO!
by USA TODAY *bestselling author*
Debra Webb

Available September 17, only from Harlequin® Intrigue®.

Love the Harlequin book you just read?

Your opinion matters.

Review this book on your favorite
book site, review site, blog or your own
social media properties and share
your opinion with other readers!

HARLEQUIN®
INTRIGUE®

THE STAKES ARE HIGHER AND THE DANGER IS BIGGER IN

MY SPY
BY DANA MARTON

A mission gone wrong forced injured soldier Jamie Cassidy to start anew…and run right into the path of deputy sheriff Bree Tridle. The sassy, sexy Texan was as determined to uncover a local money-laundering scheme as Jamie was to keep her safe from the stalker hot on her trail. When a deadly attack on Bree's home escalates the danger *and* their attraction, they must face their enemies together to save not only their country, but their one chance at love.

LAST SPY STANDING
also included in this book!

*Available September 17, 2013,
only from Harlequin® Intrigue®.*

HI69720